Jennings' Little Hut

First published in this edition 1973

To G.A.B.

© *Anthony Buckeridge, 1951*
ISBN 0 00 162142 4
PRINTED AND MADE IN GREAT BRITAIN BY
WM. COLLINS SONS AND CO. LTD.
LONDON AND GLASGOW

Jennings'
Little Hut

ANTHONY BUCKERIDGE

Collins

LONDON AND GLASGOW

Contents

CHAPTER ONE

The Squatters

IT WAS only a little hut, but Jennings was very proud of it. He crouched in the low doorway and a glow of happiness warmed him as his gaze drifted round the draughty interior.

Of course, it was still rather muddy he thought, but they could use the planks of the front door for duckboards until they had finished digging the patent drain on the marshy side of the floor. The roof was rather thin on top and the walls were on the bald side, too, but they could easily stop the wind whistling through by collecting a few more reeds and branches. And until Darbishire had finished making his famous ventilating-shaft out of that disused drain-pipe, it was just as well that they *had* got air-conditioned walls.

All around him, Jennings could hear sounds of activity as neighbouring hut-builders cocooned themselves in their reedy igloos; they had been quick to copy his idea and claim squatters' rights, but it was he who had thought it all out in the first place.

The grounds of Linbury Court Preparatory School were spacious. The main buildings were grouped round the quadrangle; then came the cricket pitches, the Headmaster's garden, and stretches of rough grassland. Past these, and reaching to the limits of the forty-acre estate, was the wood; and in the wood was the pond. It was an obliging sort of pond that seemed to ask for exciting, tracking games to be played round it, and the shrubs and bulrushes growing about its banks almost implored people to build huts in them. Jennings and Darbishire were building

5

a hut together, and they had made up their minds that it was going to be the finest residence in the whole colony, when it was finished.

It was Jennings' third term at Linbury and he was nearly eleven. He was an eager, rather impetuous boy with a wide-awake look in his eyes and a head of brown hair that no comb could keep parted for long. As he knelt on the soggy clay floor, loud metallic bangings came from an inner compartment at the far end of the hut.

"Don't kick up such a frantic hoo-hah, Darbishire," Jennings called. "Can't you hammer a bit more quietly?"

From the inner sanctum, a pink and white face, topped with fair curly hair, peered out. It was a serious face with spectacles.

"I'd like to see you do better! " it said. "It's pretty tricky making a famous prefabricated ventilating-shaft, when you've only got your shoe to hammer with. I wouldn't be surprised if it's not dangerous, too, because I've got those sort of iron horse-shoe things on my heel, and every time I wallop the drain-pipe, it sparks like a welding machine." The craftsman crawled through into the larger room, dragging his drain-pipe behind him. "There you are," he said. "It's finished now. I bet nobody else has got a patent, prefabricated ventilating-shaft in their hut."

"Neither would we, if you hadn't sat on it and bent it in the middle," replied Jennings. "I was going to get a small hunk of mirror and make it into a periscope and bung it through the roof, so's we could see people coming."

"You don't need a periscope for that," Darbishire objected. "The walls are so thin you can see people coming through them, anyhow."

"If anyone wants to come in," said Jennings, "they can wizard well use the front door. If people start coming in through the walls . . ."

"No, I didn't mean that. I meant—oh, well, never mind. Let's put the shaft up, shall we? It'll help to prop up the roof, and from outside it'll look as though we'd got a chimney. Gosh, Temple and Venables and all the other chaps will be as fed up as two coots when we show them

6

all our labour-saving gadgets. They haven't got anything half as decent as this in their huts." Darbishire's eyes sparkled behind his spectacles; the junior partner was every bit as keen as his colleague on building a hut which would be the envy of all who were invited to admire its classic architecture.

There was a small puddle in the middle of the floor, for even in June the marshy ground near the pond retained its moisture; so they knelt on small, inadequate dock-leaves and set to work to erect the shaft.

The lower end gurgled its way into the mud and the top was pushed through the sparse foliage of the roof. They knew, of course, that the drain-pipe had no air-conditioning properties to speak of, but it added tone to the place. One could say: "We've got a supersonic patent prefabricated ventilating-shaft in our hut," in the same tone that one might say: "We've got a television set in the billiard room."

"Come on," said Jennings. "Let's go and get some more reeds to block up the walls." They crawled through the low entrance and scampered down to the water's edge.

Huts of every shape and style were growing up near the bank. Some were merely leafy tents that only their owners or the ancient Picts and Scots would have described as desirable residences; others were more ambitious and had sun-parlours and twisty tunnels of bramble between one room and the next. Venables and Temple had built so low a structure that they had to crawl like snakes all the time they were inside, while Atkinson's shanty was tall enough to house a giraffe, but so narrow that the animal could never have wagged its tail.

Martin-Jones and Paterson were making a hut up a tree, and Bromwich had decided upon a semi-basement type of dwelling which sank into the earth like an elephant-trap.

Venables and Temple emerged from their hut like burrowing moles, as Jennings and Darbishire staggered past with armfuls of reeds.

"Come and see what we're doing," Jennings invited.

7

"Our hut's simply smashing—at least it will be when we've made the roof a bit thicker and drained the floor."

Venables, a tall thin boy of eleven, rose to his feet and brushed the mud from his knees. "I bet it's not so good as ours," he said. "Ours is so snug there isn't room to breathe, let alone turn round, and we have to beetle out in reverse gear, don't we, Bod?"

His friend nodded. Temple had answered to the name of Bod ever since his initials, which spelt CAT, had been altered to DOG and "shortened" to Dogsbody.

"Yes, but ours has got two rooms," argued Jennings. "A living-room in front and a small back room where Darbishire goes and invents things."

Venables and Temple left their low-built apartment and followed the pioneer squatters to the little hut.

"Here we are," said Jennings, throwing down his bundle of reeds. "This is the front door."

"Where?" asked Temple.

"Well, this is the place where it goes when it's working. We've got it on the floor at the moment—that's one of Darbishire's inventions. When you don't want it as a door you can use it as duckboards."

"I don't know about duckboards," retorted Venables, picking his way between the puddles. "You'll need stilts if it gets any wetter."

"Ah, but I've got plans to dig a special irrigation drainage canal," Darbishire explained, as the sightseers crawled in. "And actually, it's super decent to have masses of water. Supposing we were besieged—we'd be able to hold out for months. Why, we could even wash, if we felt like it!"

"And we're going to use this tin can to store the water in—it's another of Darbi's supersonic wheezes," Jennings chimed in. He rolled an empty five-gallon oil drum to the middle of the hut. "I fished it out of the pond yesterday. We can have it either as an emergency drinking supply—only you mustn't really drink it, of course, because it's a bit tadpoley—or we can use it as a patent fire-extinguisher. Just at the moment we use it as a tribal tom-tom when we feel like a spot of drum music." He performed a short percussion solo, which rumbled round the little hut like gun-fire.

The guests were deeply impressed. "Fancy Darbishire thinking all that up!" said Temple admiringly. "I'd always put you down as a bit of a wet dishcloth, Darbi—I'd no idea you were such a genius."

"Oh, I don't know," smiled the inventor, bursting with pride. "It's just a gift, I suppose." He gave a little self-conscious laugh, and blew his nose to hide his embarrassment.

The visiting squatters found that the conducted tour of the hut imposed a severe strain on the human form. Unlike their own hut, the roof was not so low that they had to crawl; but on the other hand, it was just not high enough for them to stand upright. Venables shambled about with bent knees, in a curious crouching attitude, and Temple bowed his shoulders and drooped his head so that he was unable to see anything higher than the floor, unless he stood a long way off. Darbishire was short enough to be able to prance about in an upright position, and Jennings had solved his head-room problems with cardboard knee-pads, on which he shuffled around rapidly.

The hut was circular and the main room was about six feet in diameter; from outside, it looked like a rather thin bee-hive. The hosts displayed their furniture and fittings with some pride. There was a cane-seated rustic chair which Jennings had made from broken branches and bulrushes; it was perfectly safe, provided that no one actually sat on it. There was a pair of bicycle handlebars, salvaged from the pond and now in use as a hat-stand; they were still searching hopefully for a hat to hang on it. There was a bookshelf, a bootscraper, and a brass curtain rod, and wedged tightly into the wall, Venables found a biscuit tin.

"What's this for?" he demanded.

"That's the refrigerator," Jennings explained. "At least, it will be. We're going to put a leaky tin of water on the roof, so it drips down the outside wall and keeps the fridge cool. We're saving up for a banquet, you see; we've got a pork pie already and we're keeping it till we get this

9

month's sweet rations to go with it. It'll be supersonic, won't it?"

Venables opened the biscuit tin and then shut it again quickly. "It's supersonic already," he announced. "Your pork pie's going much faster than sound—it's growing cotton-wool round the edges in spite of your air-conditioned walls."

"Never mind," said Jennings, "we can give it to the moorhens—they're not fussy. Perhaps we can get some potatoes and things later on and make a fire and actually cook them."

"We'll come and help you, if you like," Venables suggested. "I'm a pretty good cook. I made a cake at home, once. It was super! I got some flour and stuff and boiled it for three hours in a pudding cloth. Then we ate it."

"The cake, or the cloth?"

"The cake, of course. We threw the cloth away. Although actually," he admitted, for he was a truthful boy, "actually, it might have tasted better if we'd thrown away the cake and eaten the cloth."

They crawled through the hole into the small back room, and examined the half-finished arts and crafts with which Jennings and Darbishire were planning to improve their home comforts. Painted jam jars stood ready to serve as flower vases; curtains, hand-woven from bulrushes awaited a few finishing touches, and on the wall hung a sugar-sack with the words, *Welcome to Ye Oldë Worldë Huttë* picked out in a tasteful variety of colours.

"That's the door-mat," Jennings explained. "And we're doing the lettering by sticking the tops of fizzy-drink bottles through the sacking. It took us weeks to collect all those bottle tops. I had to haunt the tuck-shop like a leech."

"It's not bad," Venables admitted. "Except that you can't spell."

Jennings and Darbishire glanced at each other with superior, knowing smiles. "That just shows how much *you* know!" said Jennings. "This is an ancient rustic hut, I'd have you know, and we've been to a lot of trouble to get everything just right. And you have to put an 'e' on the ends of words because that's how they spelt it in the Stone Age. I expect we'll have finished it by next week, and it'll look fabulous outside the front door. Of course, it's not for wiping your feet on—it's just a work of art."

Venables felt that open-mouthed admiration of a rival hut had gone quite far enough. "Of course, ours will look pretty super when we've finished it," he said. "We've got all sorts of plans in mind."

"What sort of plans?" demanded Jennings.

"Oh—er, just different sorts of plans. We've thought of lots. For instance . . ." He paused, seeking desperately for just one face-saving improvement. "Well, like, say, for instance, such as a hunk of corrugated iron to make a porch with. We saw one in the pond yesterday and we're going to try and get it out."

"A corrugated iron porch!" Jennings' tone was disdainful. Corrugated iron struck a jarring, modern note amongst this old-world rusticity. There was something not quite old-English about corrugated iron.

A whistle sounded in the distance. "Come on!" said Temple. "There's Mr. Carter blowing the 'all-in'. Let's get back over the bridge before the rush hour starts."

On all sides bodies were emerging from huts as the four boys hurried towards the slope which led to higher ground. There was a quagmire at the foot of the slope where the pond had overflowed across the path, and here the pioneer hut-builders had erected the Darbishire Pontoon-Suspension Bridge.

It was an unusual feat of engineering which the inventor had conceived on the lines of the Forth Bridge, using branches and string in place of girders and rivets. But the first time it was used, it sagged so low that it floated on the water and the builders had been obliged to prop it up with pontoons made from petrol cans. By and large, it was still considered to be a suspension bridge; the only difference was that it was the traveller, and not the bridge, who was in a state of suspension as he swung himself across an awkward gap, with the aid of an over-hanging branch.

11

Single-line traffic and no overtaking was the rule, and it was this bottleneck that slowed the hurrying tide of hut builders to a snail-paced crawl. Mr. Carter's whistle sounded again—impatiently this time, as the boys awaited their turn to cross.

"Oh, gosh, this is frantic!" bemoaned Darbishire. "If we're not back when the dorm bell goes, the Head will put the pond out of bounds again. I nearly fainted with shock when he let us come over here in the first place."

"Why shouldn't we come?" demanded Temple. "After all, it's educational. Think of all the nature craft and stuff you learn by watching moorhens and tadpoles and building suspension bridges and things."

"It was jolly decent of Mr. Carter to ask the Archbeako to let us," said Jennings. "It's not often you find grown-ups who are keen on huts. They seem to turn against things like that when they get old."

"Mr. Carter's not old," protested Temple.

"Oh, he is. He's at least twenty-five or thirty. More than that, probably—say, forty-five or fifty, even. He must be pretty ancient because I happen to know he was alive in the olden days."

"He ought to be able to read your oldë worldë Stone Age huttë language, then."

"Well, not all that old, of course," Jennings amended. "But he can remember right back to the time before they'd invented jet-propelled aircraft and transistors. Why, when he was young, I don't suppose they'd ever heard of moon rockets and diesel engines and things."

In single file they picked their way across the pontoon-suspension bridge and ran full tilt past the cricket pitches. Mr. Carter was waiting for them on the quad.

Seen at close quarters, the master did not appear to be the sole surviving relic of a by-gone age that Jennings' description had suggested. He was in his early thirties—a friendly, unhurried sort of man who remained calm amidst all the excitements which ruffled the surface of boarding-school life. "How are the huts progressing?" he inquired.

"They're going fine, sir," Jennings told him. "And we're all learning masses of natural history and botany, sir."

"Really!" marvelled Mr. Carter. "Such as what?"

"Well, sir, I've learned you can cut your finger on bul-rushes and you can't keep newts out of a hut, however many anti-reptile traps you dig round it, sir."

"I see. Well, there's one point you'd better bear in mind. If anyone gets his feet wet, or falls into the pond—or even if he gets stuck in an anti-reptile trap—it will mean the end of hut building. The Head's most particular about your not getting dirty and spoiling your clothes."

"Yes, sir," chorused the hut-builders, trying to edge behind one another in their efforts to conceal muddy socks and pond-slimed shoes.

"Don't shuffle about when I'm talking," said Mr. Carter. "I'm not blind; I'm just giving you a friendly warning. You'd better be getting upstairs now—the dormitory bell's just going."

In the bathroom that evening, they could talk of nothing but huts. It was a week since they had been given permission to start building operations, but as opportunities of going over to the pond were confined to the hour before bedtime, the venture was only just beginning to take shape. But now, walls were up and roofs were on—except in a few cases where the weight of the roof had collapsed the walls—and every squatter was eager to convert his make-shift cabin into a comfortable home-from-home.

"Our hut's easily the best," Jennings proclaimed through a film of soap bubbles. "Thanks to Darbi's famous inventions, it's just like an ideal home exhibition."

"Well, I bet you haven't got a knocker and a front-door bell," retorted Atkinson, three baths away. "I've made a super bell out of a cocoa tin with pebbles in it. All I want now is a front door to hang it on, and it'll be just the job." He lay back in his bath turning the taps on and off with his toes, while his mind conjured up an endless stream of visitors queueing up to rattle pebbles in a cocoa tin.

The latest improvements were discussed in detail, above

the trickle of running taps. Martin-Jones had written home for an air-cushion and a string hammock. Rumbelow had carved a name-plate with *Cosy Nook* in letters of bark, and Binns was making a similar one, inscribed *No Hawkers*. Nuttall's hut boasted two plastic mugs and a flag-pole with a flag on it. Brown had a first-aid outfit consisting of two bandages and a corn-plaster, and Johnson had found an inner tube which could be used as a life-belt if anyone fell into the pond. Everyone was anxious to broadcast the merits of his scheme of interior decoration.

Everyone, except Bromwich. He sat in his bath rubbing carbolic soap into his thick black hair, and said nothing.

"How are you getting on, Bromo?" Jennings inquired from the next bath. "I should think it must be a bit gloomy having a hut that sinks down like an air raid shelter."

"I'm getting on all right," said Bromwich, "and I'm going to have something in my hut that none of the rest of you would think of, if you guessed for a million years."

"What?"

"Ah! You wait till you see it. It's top priority secret. My mother's coming down to take me out after chapel tomorrow, and she's bringing it with her. And when it comes it'll make your ventilating-shafts and string hammocks look pretty silly. You can have grand pianos and electric cookers and potted palms, for all I care," Bromwich went on, generously. "They still wouldn't be a patch on this thing that I'm going to have." He swallowed a great gulp of air and disappeared beneath the bath water in an attempt to break the Form 3 breath-holding record.

Bromo was like that, Jennings thought: always wanting to be a lone wolf and having a secret which no one else must know. And then, in the end, it always turned out to be such a feeble sort of secret that no one wanted to know, anyway. Still, you never knew. Perhaps he had thought of something rare, for a change; perhaps . . . Jennings' mind rambled on while his fingers sculptured the soap into a round ball. Then, with a sudden faint plop, the soap shot

14

out of his slippery hands and landed on Darbishire, who was scrambling into his pyjamas.

"Who did that?" demanded Darbishire. He peered round vaguely, but he had left his spectacles in the dormitory, and without them the room was just a blurred mass of steamy figures.

"Sorry, Darbi," called Jennings. "I was just inventing a jet-propelled soap-rocket and it got out of control. Chuck it back, please; I want to see if I can . . ."

His words were drowned by convulsive blowings and heavings as Bromwiich broke the surface of the water, like a short-winded whale coming up for air. "Phew!" he gasped. "I bet *that's* a breath-holding record. I counted thirty-seven, quite slowly. Bet you haven't guessed it, yet!"

"Guessed what?"

"This secret thing my mother's bringing down for my hut." He smiled mysteriously. "You'd like to know what it is, wouldn't you?"

"No," said Jennings, bursting with curiosity. "I wouldn't listen if you told me."

"That's all right, then," said Bromwich, "because I'm not going to."

It was not until the following week that the top-priority secret was revealed, for the next day was Sunday, and the pond was out of bounds.

Immediately after preparation on Monday evening, Jennings and Darbishire hurried across to their hut and set about thatching the balder sections of the roof. Jennings had forgotten about Bromwich and his secret, and he was rather surprised when a thick black head of hair popped up from behind the hut and a triumphant voice said: "I've got it!"

"Got what?"

"Come and see!"

The two boys followed Bromwich to his hut. The only way to enter was to lie down and slide through a hole in the reeds, for the lone wolf favoured a subterranean style of architecture. There was a straw landing-mat to break the fall of those who came in more quickly than they meant to, and then the visitor found himself in a natural hollow of the ground which had been roughly roofed in. Faint beams of light trickled through the slats of the roof, but for a moment, the guests stood blinking in the dim-lit interior, unable to see anything at all. Then Jennings saw it.

"Gosh!" he murmured. "How super-cracking-sonic! You are lucky, Bromo: I wish I'd got one!"

"Got one *what*?" demanded Darbishire, peering short-sightedly through the gloom.

"There," said Jennings. "Look!"

Balanced on a broken cake-stand in the middle of the floor, was a tank of water. And in the tank was a goldfish.

"An aquarium—golly, how wizard!" Darbishire stood on one foot and flipped his fingers with delight. "Wherever did you get that from?"

"My mother brought it down by car yesterday," Bromwich explained. "It took her years to get here. She could only drive at about four miles a fortnight, in case she spilt the water. Not bad is he?"

There was no doubt that Bromwich major was devoted to his pet. He gazed lovingly into the tank and smiled at the goldfish like a fond parent at a school concert. The goldfish champed its jaws and goggled back unwinkingly. "I wanted one of these more than anything else," the owner went on. "He's the perfect ornament for a hut like this. You can keep your air-cushions and your hammocks . . ."

"We haven't got any hammocks."

"Well, you can keep your prefabricated ventilating-shafts."

"Thank you," said Darbishire. "We were going to."

"You can keep the whole lot," cried Bromwich with fierce pride. "All I want is my fish. Elmer and I are going to settle down together and . . ."

"Who?" queried Darbishire.

"Elmer. That's my fish's name."

"Why?"

"*Why?* Well, why not? Why are you called Darbishire?"

"Oh, that's quite easy to explain. My father says that years ago our family used to be known as . . ."

"All right, all right," Jennings broke in. "We don't want your family history right back to William the Conq." He turned to the proud owner. "Thanks for showing us, Bromo. I think Elmer's super, and you'll never feel lonely now: you'll be able to sit and look at each other during the long summer evenings."

They left Bromwich to his fish and scrambled up through the doorway. As they walked back to their own hut, Jennings said: "You know, Darbi, a pet like that is just the right sort of thing for a boarding school. He can't escape, like guinea-pigs; you don't have to take him for walks and he doesn't eat much. Gosh, you can't go wrong with a goldfish, can you?"

"I bet *you* could," his friend answered. "If you were in charge of a high-spirited pet like that, I bet you'd manage to make a bish of it, somehow!" Darbishire's tone was light and bantering. He little knew how near the truth he was.

CHAPTER TWO

Last Wicket Stand

IT WAS on the following Wednesday that three boys retired to the sanatorium with mumps. The illness first raised its swollen neck among the thirteen-year-olds in the top form; by the next day it had spread to lower forms of life, and Binns, the youngest boy in the school, joined the ranks of the stricken. He would have been delighted at the idea of missing three weeks' work, if only he had not been feeling too ill to enjoy it.

"It's a swizzle," said Jennings, as they left the hut that evening. "There should have been a match against Brace-bridge on Saturday, and now they'll have to cancel it."

"Can't be helped," replied Darbishire. "Mr. Carter said this afternoon that we could have first and second XI house matches instead. You're bound to be picked, and with any luck they may put me down as scorer."

Darbishire was not a good cricketer; but with a score book in front of him he was perfectly happy to sit in the pavilion all afternoon, well away from the hurly-burly of fast bowling. More important still, the scorer had the right to tell the boys bigger than himself to move out of the light if they were blocking his view of the pitch. Sometimes, Darbishire wondered what would happen if he tried this on when he was *not* scoring.

His hopes were fulfilled. Jennings was picked to captain the Drake second XI in its match against the rival house of Raleigh, and Darbishire's name appeared on the bottom of the list as scorer. They both looked forward to a pleasant Saturday afternoon.

18

Unfortunately, they had not allowed for an unpleasant Saturday morning. Boy after boy awoke with a headache and was removed to the sick room to await the doctor's verdict. Gaps appeared in the house cricket teams and the rival captains dived lower and lower into the pool of cricketing talent in their efforts to find substitutes.

Jennings stood by the notice board just before lunch watching Stoddington, his house captain, making last-minute alterations to the teams in his charge. Parslow had just gone upstairs to Matron to report a sudden tenderness below the ears, and there seemed no one left to replace him. In despair, Stoddington's pencil scratched through the word scorer, and Darbishire, for the first time in his life, was promoted to the ranks of the Drake house second XI.

"Gosh!" exclaimed Jennings in amazement. "Greatest news since the landing of Julius Cæsar—Old Darbi's been picked at last! And in my team, too; I must go and tell him. Get off my runway, Venables—I'm a jet-propelled strato-cruiser taking off on a super important mission. Eee-ow-ow . . . Eee-ow-ow!" He strato-cruised along to the common room, where he found Darbishire hard at work with drawing-book and paint brush.

"What do you think, Darbi?" he began, giving his friend a hearty pat on the back. "Great news!"

"You great crumbling ruin," protested the artist, recoiling from the hearty pat. "Now look what you've done! You've made me do a smudge on this painting I was doing to hang up in the hut."

Jennings looked down at the work of art. It was a tasteful landscape, with cows grazing in the middle distance and an express train hurtling over a flimsy wooden bridge in the foreground. And it was still very wet.

"Sorry," Jennings apologised. "It won't matter, will it?"

"It jolly well *will* matter! I was just painting the grass when you jogged me, and now I've got a cow with a green face."

"Never mind," Jennings consoled him. "You can pretend it isn't feeling very well—that'll explain why it's a bit off

19

colour. Anyway, I've got an urgent message for you; you've been picked for the second XI house match."

Darbishire heard the news with mixed feelings. It was an honour such as he had never dreamed of, but he was a little uncertain whether he would be able to rise to the occasion.

"Oh, well," he said, "this is my big chance, I suppose. My father says that Fate knocks once at the door of every man." For a moment he lapsed into a daydream of late cuts and off drives; of a glorious six over the bowler's head and tumultuous cheers from the pavilion. Then, with an effort, he brought his mind back to the realms of probability. "And you mean to say my name's actually up on the board?"

"Yes. In block letters."

"And not just as scorer?"

"No. Square leg and number eleven in the batting order."

"Golly, I wonder if they'd give me the list afterwards, so's I could send it to my father. Let's go and have a look at it; this sort of thing doesn't happen every day, does it!"

Together they strato-cruised back along the corridor and touched down by the crowd round the notice board. Darbishire spoke with the authority that his place in the team demanded: "Shift out of my light, Atkinson," he said. "You're blocking my view of the team."

It was Darbishire's performances in the junior house match that made Jennings decide to give his friend some intensive coaching. Raleigh batted first, and as the Drake bowling tended towards long-hops on the leg side, Darbishire was kept busy. Not that he actually saved any boundaries, but it was useful to have a willing fielder on the spot to retrieve the ball from the hedge.

The bowling strength of both teams had been badly affected by the absentees in the sick bay. Jennings and Bromwich had to bowl throughout the innings almost without relief, and after the first hour's play they were tired and unable to maintain their length.

"Oh, gosh, Bromo," bemoaned Silly Mid Off, "can't you do better than that? That's two wides this over!"

"Sorry," returned Bromwich. "It's that bump on the pitch. Whenever I do a leg-break it turns it into a wide on the off."

"Well, do off-breaks, then."

"That's no good either. The last off-break that pitched on the bump nearly brained the square leg umpire."

Mr. Hind, a tall thin man with a quiet voice, was in charge of the junior game. "If things go on like this," he observed sadly, "you'd better get a scarecrow with outstretched arms to umpire at the bowler's end. I'm a trifle weary of signalling wides."

He sat on his shooting-stick and looked enviously across at Mr. Carter who was umpiring the senior match on an adjoining pitch. There, at any rate, one could be sure of good length bowling and promising batting strokes.

Jennings tried a change of bowlers, but it was not a success and after a few overs he put himself on to bowl at Mr. Hind's end. The telegraph board showed 66 runs for seven wickets, and the captain encouraged his men for an all-out effort. "Only three more chaps to get out," he told them. "Let's see if we can get the whole side out for under seventy."

The word spread round the fielding side. "Special effort, chaps. Everyone on their toes!"

Jennings swung his arm round like a propeller before starting his run up to the wicket. It was his method of generating current for an extra-special delivery, and though it did not always succeed, he felt it was worth trying.

This time, it worked. The ball pitched on the little bump and shot forward to hit the stumps at grass-top level: and the Raleigh batsman retired to the pavilion complaining about balls which cut through the turf like plough-shares. Jennings' luck held. His next ball was wide of the off stump and the new batsman prodded at it vaguely. By chance he touched it and the wicket-keeper held an easy catch. Two wickets in two balls! The Drake fielders went wild with delight, smiting one another on the back and dancing ungainly ballet steps round the wicket.

"66 for nine," said Jennings happily. "If I can get

Thompson out this ball, it'll be a hat trick and they won't get seventy after all. Gosh, I've never done the hat trick in a house match yet."

Thompson always played the same stroke to every ball he received; he took a step backwards and swung his bat as though scything a field of corn. As Jennings' first ball hurtled down the pitch towards him, Thompson played his unvarying stroke and the ball rose from his bat and curved gently away towards the leg boundary.

Atkinson was umpiring at square leg. Unlike Mr. Hind, he had no shooting-stick, so he sat on a reversed cricket bat instead. He ducked, and the ball lobbed over his head, straight into the hands of the square leg fielder.

If it had been a difficult catch, Darbishire would not have felt so unhappy about missing it. But it wasn't. The ball sank gently into his hands and his spirits soared in triumph: then, the ball dropped and his spirits with it. He stared aghast, unable to believe his eyes. For a second he had actually felt the ball nestling in his palms, and now the beastly thing had slipped through his fingers like an eel. It was incredible . . . It was the end of everything . . . It was . . . !

"Darbishire!" yelled the wicket-keeper, dancing behind the stumps like a cat on hot bricks.

The fielder came to with a jerk and saw that the batsmen were running. Perhaps he could run them out. Perhaps, if he threw very straight he could . . . He swung his arm back hard for the return throw and the ball flew out of his fingers and landed in the hedge behind him. Mr. Hind signalled a boundary and four more runs went up on the board.

"Gosh, Darbishire, you are a ruin!" grumbled the Drake fielders as they gathered in the pavilion after the Raleigh innings had closed for 84 runs.

"Sorry," said Darbishire humbly.

"You bished up Jennings' hat trick and just chucked runs away," said Cover Point. "Messing up that throw in, after missing the easiest catch I ever saw. Anyone could have held a soft one like that."

22

"Anyone except Darbishire," amended Second Slip. "He couldn't even catch mumps with a shrimping net."

"Shut up," said Jennings, coming to his friend's rescue. "We can't all be Test Match cricketers. You may be good at one thing and Darbishire may be good at another."

"Such as what?"

"Well, like, say, for instance, inventing things. He's smashing at that. And he can do a better imitation of a train going through a tunnel than anyone else in the school."

"Thanks, Jen," said Darbishire gratefully. "I'm sorry about bishing up that catch off your bowling, though."

"That's all right," Jennings replied generously. "He wouldn't have been out even if you *had* caught it. It was a 'no ball'."

The Drake innings opened disastrously, and three wickets fell for only a dozen runs. Then Jennings went in and stopped the rot. This was only to be expected, for he would have been picked for the senior game if his own team had not been so short of bowlers. Batsmen came and went, and when 50 runs appeared on the board, Jennings had made 20 of them. Drake took heart, and the tail of the team wagged strenuously as it added a few more runs for each wicket.

The score was 79 for eight when Darbishire realised, with a qualm of misgiving, that he was the next man in. He found a pad and strapped it on; the buckle was missing at the bottom, but there was no time to do anything about it, and he was still searching for a second pad when a burst of cheering from the field announced that the ninth wicket had fallen.

Darbishire glanced at the score board and noticed that the score had crept up to 83. Jennings was still at the wicket, playing a captain's innings.

"Buck up, Darbi—you're in," announced Fine Leg.

"I can't go yet—I've only got one pad."

"Never mind about that. You won't be there all that long. Just stick in and let Jennings get the runs. Unless, of course, you get an easy one—then you can have a crack at it."

The last man in swallowed hard; it was stupid to talk about his getting an easy one. Things like that never happened to him.

"Go on, Darbi—don't hang about," said Mid On. "My nerves won't stand this suspense much longer." Two runs to make! The atmosphere pulsed with excitement.

Darbishire grabbed a bat and a pair of gloves and strode boldly towards the wicket, his single, broken pad flapping uncomfortably about his ankle. It was not until he reached the crease that he remembered that he had not taken his blazer off.

"Just a mo, please," he said, and fumbled at the buttons with his padded fingers, while the fielders shifted about restlessly. When the buttons were undone, the blazer slipped off his shoulders easily enough, but it was rather tight at the wrist and try as he would, he could not force his sleeves over his batting-gloves.

"Sorry about this," he apologised, with his arms pinioned behind his back. "I'm afraid I'll have to take my gloves off first."

The Raleigh fielders seethed with impatience. They, too, could hardly wait to get on with the game.

"It's no good," said Darbishire, a few moments later, "I can't get my gloves off behind my back; I'll have to get my blazer on properly, first."

"Here, let me help!" Jennings marched down the pitch to lend a hand. "We can't possibly wait while you mess about putting your gloves on and off. Bend forward and hold your arms out and I'll strip it off, inside out." He seized the hem of the blazer and heaved it over his friend's head, but again they were baffled by the tight cuffs. The batsman's head and neck were shrouded in blazer, and soon calls for help came from within.

"Hey, whoa, stop! I'm stuck and I can't breathe." He floundered helplessly about like the back legs of a panto-mime horse looking for its partner.

"What's the matter?" asked Jennings, popping his head into the flannelly tunnel from the open end.

"This is ghastly," said Darbishire. "My cap's got stuck in the armhole and my glasses have come off. I think they've slipped down inside my shirt."

"Keep still—I'll see if I can get them for you."

There were queer movements inside the blazer, as though two old-fashioned photographers were sharing one head-covering between them. Then one of the headless bodies backed out of the tunnel and stood breathing lungfuls of fresh air.

"Oh, for goodness' sake get a move on!" called Venables from the bowler's end, while the rest of the fielders hopped up and down and waved their arms in wild gestures of frustration.

At last Darbishire was ready to face the bowling. The fielders closed in, prepared to pounce like hawks if the batsman should spoon up an easy catch. They looked at one another and smiled craftily; they had met batsmen like Darbishire before.

Just as the bowler started his run, Darbishire realised that he had strapped his pad on to the wrong leg. But he could not change it now, unless he stopped the game and removed his gloves again, and he decided that this might not go down well with the other players.

He was pondering the problem when the ball came hurtling towards him. It was one of Venables' special deliveries, noted for pace rather than accuracy. The ball flashed past the batsman, past the stumps, past the wicket-keeper's clutching gloves and sped away with First Slip in pursuit.

Darbishire turned and watched it. "Gosh," he observed to the wicket-keeper. "That was a fast one, wasn't it! I didn't even see it coming. Look at old Bod legging after it like blinko. I bet he . . ."

"Quick, run!" yelled a voice behind him and, turning, the batsman found that Jennings had arrived from the bowling end. For one agonised moment they both stood in the same crease, while Temple fielded the ball and threw it back towards the pitch.

"Get back!" cried Darbishire.

"I can't. I've got here, now. Run!"

Darbishire ran, but without much hope. Temple's throw had reached the middle of the pitch and the cover point seized it and hurled it with all his force at the bowler's wicket. It missed the stumps by half an inch and streaked away past mid on. Darbishire breathed again and didn't stop running until he reached Mr. Hind, five yards behind the wicket.

"Gosh, sir, did you see that?" he asked the umpire. "I thought I'd had it that time, sir. If only it had been half a . . ."

"Darbishire!" yelled the Drake team from the pavilion. "Run up, you idiot, run up!" They clutched their heads and writhed in nervous despair.

"Wake up!" said Mr. Hind. "There's another run on the overthrow, if you're quick."

"Oh, gosh, yes, of course!"

Jennings had almost reached the crease again before his partner was off the mark on his second run, and this time Darbishire's luck was out. Three-quarters of the way along the pitch, he stepped on the end of his flapping pad and tripped himself up. The next second the bails were whipped off and the match was over.

Darbishire rose slowly to his feet, numb with misery. If only he had been more alert, this would never have happened. His big chance had come and he had not lasted long enough to face two balls. What would his father say? What were his team-mates thinking?

Judging from the noise his team-mates were making, they were taking it very well. They were waving pads and bats in the air and shouting themselves hoarse. Jennings ran up and slapped his partner on the back. "Well done," he said. "Jolly good effort!"

"Well done?" queried Darbishire. "But I didn't do anything except get run out first ball."

"What does that matter?" returned Jennings. "We won

26

the match, didn't we? We'd crossed on that last run before you went *doyng* on your face, so that makes our score 85."

"Oh yes, of course, I'd forgotten about that. And it was our last-wicket stand that did the trick, wasn't it?"

"That's right. And you got the winning run without even touching the ball!"

Darbishire beamed with delight. "It sounds super when you put it like that," he said. "I bet my father will be ever so pleased when I write and tell him."

They entered the pavilion amidst a salvo of cheers. In point of fact, the applause was for Jennings who had saved the game with a determined 33 not out, but the number eleven batsman could not resist the temptation to bask in the reflected glory. He raised his cap and smiled modestly.

After all, he had been to a lot of trouble to score that bye.

CHAPTER THREE

Operation "Exercise"

THERE WAS no evening preparation on Saturdays, and after tea Jennings and Darbishire sped away to the hut.

Jennings had decided to make a broom out of twigs, but first it would be necessary to drain the floor so that it was dry enough to be swept. No sooner had he started work than he heard his name being called, and galloping footsteps approached from the suspension bridge. It was Atkinson, an excitable boy of ten, who occupied a hut near the water's edge.

"Oh, there you are, Jen," he cried, as he charged through the undergrowth. "Bromo's got the mumps!"

"Bad luck!" said Jennings. "I thought his bowling was a bit off colour this afternoon."

"Yes, it's ozard, isn't it! He went up to Matron just after the house match, and he's sent you an urgent message via Matron, via me, to you. He wants you to look after his goldfish. He's as sick as mud at having to leave it behind, because he's so devoted to it."

"I've noticed that," chimed in Darbishire emerging from the hut. "He just *lives* for that fish. And so he should, really, because poor old Elmer's got no one else in the whole world, except Bromo. He's its next-of-kin, as you might say."

"Can't he take it up to the san with him?" suggested Jennings.

"Gosh, no!" protested Atkinson. "It might catch mumps, and a goldfish with swollen gills would look ghastly. Of course, it may be mumpy already, as Bromo's been looking

28

after it. Might be a good wheeze to stick a label on the tank—*Beware of Mumps. Do not touch.* Anyway, will you take the job on?"

Bromwich had a younger brother in the lowest form, but he was considered to be too young to bear such a heavy responsibility. As Atkinson pointed out: "You need a Form Three-er, at least, to take on a job like this. A Form One-er would be bound to make a bish of it, and besides you and Darbi have had mumps already, so you won't go teetering off to the san before Bromo gets back."

Jennings pondered for a moment. Taking care of a fish who boasted a next-of-kin was a serious business and not to be undertaken lightly. At the same time, it was gratifying to think that he had been chosen for this position of trust. Clearly, it was his duty to shoulder this burden so that Bromwich could enjoy his mumps with an easy mind.

"All right," he said, "but I don't know much about gold-fish. What do they eat?"

"That's easy; they eat eggs."

"Don't be such a prehistoric remains, Atkinson," said Jennings curtly. "They'd never be able to crack the shells."

"Not hens' eggs, you ruin—ants' eggs. They love them."

"Oh, yes, of course," said Jennings, and wondered how Elmer would like his eggs prepared. Boiled? Scrambled? Perhaps if he was sickening for mumps a little raw egg would be just the thing. In that case, all they would have to do would be to find an ant and persuade it to lay an egg.

But there was no need for this. When they slithered into Bromwich's semi-basement to take charge of Elmer, they found a tin of ready-made fish food and a flower pot containing a culture of small white worms: this, obviously, was Elmer's meat ration.

"I wonder if we ought to feed him right away," queried Jennings. "He looks pretty hungry to me. Look how he's champing his jaws."

"All goldfish do that," replied Darbishire. "It's the same as chewing the cud. They're rather like cows in that way."

Very carefully, they carried the tank and the food back to their own hut. Elmer would be happier, they decided, in an up-to-date, air-conditioned apartment than he would be in the dim-lit gloom of the Bromwich elephant trap.

For some days, Jennings and Darbishire tended Elmer as though he were one of the family. They became acutely fish conscious; they put the tank outside the hut door on pleasant evenings so that Elmer might enjoy the waning sunshine; on dull evenings, they kept him indoors. They spent hours in preparing him tasty snacks and watching him eat them; and Elmer, from his tank, would see blurred faces beyond the glass with mouths which opened and shut in time with his own.

"We ought to send Bromo a news bulletin," Jennings decided at the end of a week. "He may be getting a bit anxious."

"Good wheeze," Darbishire agreed. "You write it while I put him out for his airing. Or do you think he ought to stay in tonight? There's no sun to speak of and it might rain."

"Don't be such a crumbling ruin, Darbi. Considering he's swimming about in cold water all the time, a few drops of rain aren't going to make him much wetter."

"Maybe not," Darbishire demurred, "but the wind's a bit fresh, and we don't want him to get in a draught."

"That's all right: the cold water will keep the wind off. Don't fuss so, Darbi—you're like an old hen with a chicken. Elmer knows how to look after himself; he's a jolly clever little fish."

"So he should be," said Darbishire, as he carried the tank through the doorway. "They say fish is good for the brain, so if you're fish all over, like Elmer, you ought to be fairly bursting with intelligence."

They finished the news bulletin before they went to bed and despatched it to the sanatorium, via Matron.

"Elmer is keeping fit and not fretting," it read. "Has hearty appetite and drinks like a fish. Spends all day doing the breast stroke backwards. Have told him you will be back soon, so don't worry."

Bromwich major was extremely pleased with the news bulletin, and pinned it on the wall above his bed.

There was always plenty to do at the little hut, and a few evenings later, when Darbishire was on the roof, thatching a recent leak, he was troubled to hear waves of song wafting out through the front door, while occasional snatches filtered through the thin patches in the western wall. The tune was *John Brown's Body*, but the words were Jennings' own:

"If triangles are equal, they are said to be congruent,
"If triangles are equal, they are said to be congruent,
"If triangles are equal, they are said to be congruent,
And the angles at the base of an isosceles triangle are
   equal."

The last line required a great deal of practice and the soloist started again. "If triangles are equal . . ."

When Darbishire could stand the song no longer, he crawled to where the ventilating-shaft stretched its stately neck into the air and shouted down it: "Pack it up, Jen, for heaven's sake! What's the idea of kicking up that ghastly hoo-hah?"

The drain-pipe had been in use as a speaking tube for some days, and Jennings had fitted a home-made two-way ear-trumpet at a convenient height from the ground. "Don't get rattled, Darbi," his voice boomed back up the tube. "It's my new way of learning geometry. It's easier if you put it to music."

"Yes, but—good gracious, why do geom in your spare time?" Darbishire's feelings were outraged.

"Don't you remember what Mr. Wilkins told us when he gave us that test last week? He said the whole form had made a frightful bish and he was going to test us again, tomorrow."

"Yes, but all the same . . ."

"Mind you, I'm not going to make a habit of working too much in my spare time, but I haven't been getting on too well with Old Wilkie lately, so I thought if I composed a special geom song, he'd see how keen I was."

Darbishire considered this. Mr. Wilkins had a temperament like a volcano. He could be pleasant enough when he chose, but at other times his mood was uncertain. Some unguarded remark would lead to earth tremors and rumblings deep down inside the crater, and the next moment the volcano would erupt, pouring its angry lava in all directions and leaving a trail of desolation and detentions in its wake.

"M'yes," Darbishire said thoughtfully. "Not a bad idea. He might let us all sing it in class. How does it go?"

They held a rehearsal—Darbishire kneeling on the roof and bawling the words down the drain-pipe, while Jennings sang into the shaft from below and accompanied the duet with drum music on the water-supply-cum-fire extinguisher.

As they were practising the difficult last line for the tenth time, Jennings broke off and called out: "Hey, that's enough, Darbi; we're frightening Elmer. He's carrying on like a submarine out of control."

"What's he doing?"

"I don't quite know. He keeps going to action stations and submerging all in one breath. Come down and see for yourself—I don't like the look of this at all."

Elmer was certainly in a lively mood. He darted to one end of his tank and then, with a sudden flip of his tail that rippled the surface and disturbed the pond-weed, he shot away to the other end and started the performance all over again. He seemed so far removed from his usual placid self, that the boys became worried.

"It can't be because he's hungry," said Jennings, "and if our famous duet upset him, there's no need for him to go on hoofing about now that we've stopped."

Darbishire consulted Bromwich's little book on the care of goldfish. He read through the symptoms of every ailment that could possibly attack the scaly inhabitant of a glass tank, but nothing seemed to fit the facts. And it couldn't be that he had caught mumps from his owner, he decided as he put the book down, for none of Matron's patients had carried on in that extraordinary way before departing for the sanatorium.

32

"I don't think he's ill at all," said Jennings. "He's just feeling restless and wants a spot of exercise. After all, if you had to live in a titchy little tank, that there wasn't room to swing a cat in, you'd get a bit browned-off."

"I should be a jolly sight more browned-off if someone *did* start swinging cats," retorted Darbishire. "Still, perhaps it is a bit cruel keeping him cooped up. It's a pity he isn't a dog—then we could take him for walks on the lead."

"Gosh, yes," Jennings exclaimed. "Why not!"

"Don't be such a bogus ruin, Jen. You can't take a fish for a walk."

"No, but we could let him have a decent swim. Not in the pond, of course—it's too muddy and he might get bitten by a moorhen. But we could let him do a couple of lengths in the swimming-bath—he'd love that!"

"We-ell," said Darbishire doubtfully, for the suggestion bristled with snags, "if we did that, how would we get him out again? This needs thinking out carefully."

Seldom had the welfare of a goldfish been discussed in such loving detail. Elmer's health and happiness, his imagined likes and dislikes were all carefully considered as the plan to give him a worth-while treat gradually took shape. Finally, it was decided that he should be placed in Darbishire's butterfly-net and lowered into the swimming-bath. Jennings could then walk slowly along the edge, while Elmer swam beside him in the net. He would be free to revel in his change of surroundings, yet unable to escape or take a wrong turning. As Darbishire pointed out, it would be rather like catching shrimps.

"But when can we do it?" he queried. "It wouldn't be safe to give him his exercise while everyone else is splashing about, and we're not allowed to go to the bath at any other time."

"I vote we do it immediately after prep tomorrow," said Jennings. "There won't be anyone there because swimming is in the morning on Tuesdays. And I know where the key's kept; it's on a hook outside the staff room door."

"There'll be an awful hoo-hah if anyone finds out. You

know the rule about not going in the bath without permish," objected Darbishire.

"But we're not going *in* the bath, you ancient remains!
It's Elmer who's going to do that. We're going to stay nice
and dry and walk along like barge horses on the towpath."

The whistle sounded in the distance and the boys wended
their way back to the school buildings. "Now, don't forget," said Jennings, as they queued up for the suspension
bridge. "Directly after prep tomorrow evening; we'll have
masses of time before the dorm bell. I'll collect Elmer and
you get your butterfly net, and we'll get cracking on Exercise Goldfish."

"Not *Exercise* Goldfish," corrected Darbishire. "You
mean, *Operation* Goldfish. You only call it Exercise when
it's a practice, and this is the real thing."

"Well, in this case, the real thing is to give Elmer some
exercise, so we'll call it 'Operation Exercise'. Buck up,
Darbi, it's your turn for the bridge."

Form 3 sat a little uneasily in their desks the following
afternoon, waiting for Mr. Wilkins to arrive. In front of
them were their geometry exercise books, marked with impatient squiggles of red ink, and bearing terse comments
in the margin. Last week's test had not been a success.

Venables said enviously: "I wish I'd got mumps; I don't
know this stuff any better now than I did last week and I
only got six marks out of ten. How many did you get,
Darbi?"

"Well, as a matter of fact," Darbishire apologised. "I
had rather an off day last Tuesday and I only got four."

"Only *four!*" echoed Jennings incredulously from the
row behind. "I should have thought you could have done
better than that, Darbi. Four out of ten—gosh, that's
ozard!" He leaned forward and flicked over the pages of
his friend's book. "And look, Old Wilkie's written *Gross
Carelessness* in the margin. Golly, Darbi, that's pretty
feeble. I bet your father would have something to say about
that!"

Darbishire pinkened. It was admittedly a lapse, for he

usually managed to hold his own in Mr. Wilkins' class; and the Rev. Percival Darbishire would certainly not be at a loss for words if he heard that his son, Charles Edwin Jeremy, had failed to make the grade. Annoyed, he picked up Jennings' book to see how much better his friend had fared. Then his eyes opened wide in indignation.

"Well, I like that!" he cried. "You've only got *two*, Jennings! Trying to make out that yours was better than mine!"

"I didn't," Jennings defended himself. "I only said four out of ten was pretty feeble. Especially when you've got *Gross Carelessness* in the margin."

"Well, you've got *Carelessness* on yours, too."

"Ah, but yours is *Gross*. That's much worse! I bet you a million pounds it is."

"And I bet you a million pounds it isn't."

"Right-o," said Jennings. "I'll ask Old Wilkie when he comes in."

He had not long to wait.

Along the corridor and into the classroom strode Mr. Wilkins, and his footsteps could not have echoed more loudly if he had been wearing divers' boots. He was a large man, quite young and full of an energy which over-flowed in a torrent of restless activity.

"Right," he boomed, as he swung the door to behind him with a crash. "All ready for the test? Question one: What are congruent triangles? Question two: What are alternate angles? Question three: . . ."

"Oh, sir!" protested the class, searching feverishly for pens and rulers. "Not so fast, sir!"

"Can't wait all day," Mr. Wilkins rattled on. "There's work to be done. Ten questions: anyone not getting more than seven right stays in tomorrow afternoon. Question three: . . ."

Jennings put up his hand. "Please, sir, shall we number them, 'one to ten', sir?"

"Of course. How else could you do it? Question three: . . ." Mr. Wilkins paused and looked hard at Jennings. "Oh, yes, Jennings—that reminds me. If you don't do very much better this time, there's going to be trouble. Your answers last week were deplorable; I've never seen such an appalling example of rank sloth and indolence."

"That's what I wanted to ask you, sir." After all, there was a million-pound wager at stake. "Is rank worse than gross, sir? I mean, wasn't Darbishire's equally rank, sir?"

"I think he means don't they both rank equally, sir," suggested Darbishire, helpfully.

"They were both bad," said Mr. Wilkins. "Nothing to choose between them."

"But, sir," Jennings persisted, "Darbishire's must have been worse than mine, because a gross is a hundred and forty-four, isn't it, sir?"

"I—I—what on earth's that got to do with it?"

"Well, sir, gross carelessness must be a hundred and forty-four times worse than ordinary carelessness, surely, sir."

"I—I—Corwumph!" barked Mr. Wilkins. "I haven't come here to listen to a lot of nonsense. I've come here to find out how much you know about congruent triangles."

"Oh, I know quite a lot, sir. I made up a song about them. It goes to the tune of . . ."

"I don't want to hear a song; I want to get on with the test. Question three . . ."

The test proceeded briskly. Too briskly for some of them, and Mr. Wilkins grew extremely impatient with boys who asked him to repeat question six when he was about to announce question ten. At last it was finished and the books were collected and laid upon the master's desk.

For the second half of the lesson, Mr. Wilkins went further into the question of triangles which were similar to one another in all respects. He invented a problem about a man who lived in a village with the unlikely name of *A*, and who wanted to cross a river to another village which rejoiced in the improbable name of *B*. It seemed that, by walking a measured distance to the west and taking two bearings from a church dedicated to Saint *C*, the traveller was constructing two invisible triangles which enabled him to work out the breadth of the river *D*.

All this Mr. Wilkins demonstrated on the blackboard, while Darbishire came to the conclusion that the only thing wrong with his pontoon-suspension bridge was its lack of congruent triangles.

Jennings' mind, however, was not wholly concentrated on the problem on hand. Dimly, he wondered why this traveller was drawing dotted lines all over the countryside, and not merely on the bends of main roads; but in the main his thoughts were of Elmer and Operation Exercise. Bromo would be ever so pleased when he heard of the care and devotion which was being lavished on his next-of-kin. He might even . . . Jennings came to with a start, for Mr. Wilkins was speaking to him.

"What have I just been saying, Jennings?"

"You said that if you knew all about similar triangles, it helped you to cross a river, sir."

"Quite right!" For a moment Mr. Wilkins had thought that the boy had not been paying attention, but it seemed that he was mistaken. "And how exactly would you go about it?" he inquired.

Jennings thought desperately. "Well, sir, I suppose you'd make big wooden ones, so that you could sit on one triangle and paddle across with the other."

"I—I—Corwumph! Are you trying to be funny?"

"No, sir, honestly, sir." And honestly, he wasn't.

"But you—you *silly* little boy, how could you . . . ? You haven't been following the problem at all. Very well, we'll see how much you knew in the test." He took Jennings' book from the pile and glanced through the answers. "H'm; seven out of ten. I'll set you an exercise to do tomorrow afternoon."

"Oh, but, sir, you said I'd be all right, if I got seven."

"I said if you got *more* than seven," returned Mr. Wilkins. "And I might even have let you off with seven, if I thought you'd been trying for the rest of the lesson. But your conduct all afternoon has been verging on the insolent. As soon as I came in the door, you started twittering about gross carelessness being something to do with the multiplication table, and your answer about the

37

traveller crossing the river was nothing short of impertinence. Come to me after the lesson and I'll give you
something to keep you busy tomorrow afternoon; and if I
get one more facetious reply to a question of mine, I'll—
I'll—well, you'd better look out."

Darbishire did his best to comfort his friend after the
lesson. "Never mind, Jen. Old Wilkie will soon get over it.
My father says that it's always darkest just before the
dawn and . . ."

"Yes, but it's a jolly swizzle," Jennings declared. "I
wasn't trying to be funny. I daren't open my mouth now,
in case he thinks I'm being insolent; and that'll lead to
another row, so that's a swizzle multiplied by a swizzle—
it's a double swizzle."

"No, it's a swizzle squared—not a double swizz," Darbishire pointed out. "For instance, double twelve is only
twenty-four, but twelve squared is a gross."

"Well, that proves what I said in class," Jennings
answered warmly. "If it works with swizzles, it's the same
with carelessness, so you owe me a million pounds."

But very soon his mood became more cheerful; the
punishment would not have to be done until the following
afternoon, so it would not interfere with Elmer's swim
which was scheduled to take place that evening.

CHAPTER FOUR

Elmer Finds a Loophole

OPERATION "EXERCISE" did not work out quite as they had planned it. Shortly after evening preparation, when there was still a clear half-hour before bedtime, Jennings staggered round the corner to the indoor swimming-bath with the goldfish tank in his arms. Darbishire was waiting for him with his butterfly net and the key, and furtively they let themselves in.

Elmer was no longer showing signs of restlessness. He remained quite still near the bottom of his tank, and only the occasional flapping of a fin told them that he was awake.

Darbishire was rather worried now that the time for action had arrived and he would have been more than willing to call the whole thing off. But Jennings would not hear of it; apart from the pleasure which Elmer would certainly derive from swimming a couple of brisk lengths, Jennings was intensely curious to know whether the experiment would be a success.

"After all," he argued, "Elmer's been putting on a lot of weight lately with all that food we've been giving him, and Bromo wouldn't like it if he got too fat. So I vote we give him a quick dip and let him do a length or two just to get his weight down."

"All right, then," Darbishire agreed, and held his net at the ready. "Hadn't we better start off in the shallow end?"

"Why? You don't think he'll feel nervous if he's out of his depth, do you?"

"Maybe *he* won't, but *I* shall."

39

Carefully, the fish was transferred to the butterfly net and lowered into the water. Jennings held the handle and moved slowly along the edge of the bath. It was a great success to start with and, as Jennings pointed out, everything was going swimmingly and Elmer would have taken the situation in his stride, if he had had anything to stride with.

Darbishire lowered his voice to a respectful whisper: "I expect he's wondering where he's got to, don't you? He had a sort of puzzled look on his face when I popped him in the net."

"I bet he's enjoying the exercise," Jennings replied. "And Bromo will be ever so pleased because he won't be nearly so fat when he comes down."

"Oh, he will," protested Darbishire. "He's bound to be fatter after lying in bed for three weeks."

"No, you ancient ruin; I meant the fish, not Bromo!" Jennings laughed aloud at the absurdity of such a misunderstanding. "Ha-ha-ha! You are a bazooka, Darbi. You thought I meant Bromo: ha-ha-ha!"

"And you really meant Elmer!" Darbishire joined in, and waves of hearty laughter echoed hollowly from the high roof of the building.

"Gosh, that was funny," laughed Jennings. "I must remember to tell Venables. You thought I meant—ha-ha-ha —and all the time I really meant—ha-ha-h . . . Glumph!" The hearty laughter stalled in mid-burst and was followed by a cry of anguish. "Oh, gosh, quick, Darbi! The fish— it's gone!"

"What! It can't have."

Jennings jerked the net clear of the water. It was empty. For some seconds they stood staring in horrified amazement while little driblets of water trickled down the mesh and dripped back into the bath. Then, when the first impact of the shock was over and the boys inspected the net at close quarters, they found a medium-sized hole in the bottom.

"Oh, heavens, Bromo will never forgive us if anything happens to Elmer," moaned Darbishire.

"He can't have swum far yet; let's see if we can see him," said Jennings. "The water's a bit dirty, though. We *would* wait till it's nearly time to have it changed—I can't see the bottom at all!"

The water was certainly cloudy. The bath was a small one, and Robinson, the odd-job man, changed the water every three weeks: and judging by the state of it on that fateful Tuesday evening, the bath was more than ready for its three-weekly renewal.

Jennings and Darbishire knelt down and peered into the murky depths. Once, Jennings caught a glimpse of a golden streak near the surface, but the fish was more than an arm's length from the side. Jennings grabbed the net, and leant over the side while Darbishire grabbed his friend's ankles, but by that time Elmer was out of range and out of sight.

"I wonder whether we could lure him to the side with bait," Jennings pondered. "Go and fetch the fish-food and that flower-pot with the worms in, Darbi, while I stop here on guard."

His friend returned some minutes later with the bait. He had also brought an armful of pond-weed in the hope that Elmer would be attracted by the foliage he knew so well. It was rather muddy, for Darbishire had gathered it fresh from the pond, but he dropped it into the bath and hoped for the best. Jennings sprinkled half a tin of fish-food on the water and submerged the flower-pot beneath the surface in the butterfly net.

It was all in vain. No fin rippled the water, no jaws rose to take the bait.

"Oh gosh, this is ozard!" cried Darbishire in despair. "Why do these frantic hoo-hahs always have to pick on us to happen to? My father knows a proverb which says you should never meddle . . ."

"All right, all right," retorted Jennings sharply, for he, too, was feeling anything but happy. "I've heard quite enough about what your father always says about everything. It'd be a jolly sight more to the point if he knew a proverb about how to get a goldfish out of a swimming bath."

"Well, he does know one about there being as many good fish in the sea as ever came out."

"Honestly, Darbi! If you can't think of anything better to say than . . ."

The shrilling of a distant bell cut into his words, and miserably he said: "Oh, gosh! There's the dorm bell. We'll have to go."

"But we can't go," objected Darbishire. "Bromo would have a relapse if anything happened to Elmer. And we can't ask Mr. Carter or anyone to help because of being in here without permish. Oh, goodness, why did we have to go and lose him?"

"It was your fault for having a net with a hole in it," Jennings answered. "Anyway, we haven't lost him because we know where he is. He won't drown and he can't get out, so we'll leave him in the bath tonight and come down before breakfast tomorrow and have another go. We're bound to catch him then."

"All right, then," Darbishire agreed, "but we shall have to think of a better method. What we really need is a tennis net or something we could drag along the bath like a deep sea trawler."

They hid the empty tank in one of the cubicles, and Darbishire took his net with him so that he could repair the hole. In case Elmer should feel hungry Jennings emptied the rest of the fish food on to the floating bait, and while he was doing so, he accidentally knocked the flower-pot into the bath. As it sank to the bottom, it added its earthy mixture to the already discoloured water.

They were replacing the key outside the staff room when Atkinson came hurrying along. "Oh, there you are, Jen," he said. "I've just had another message from Bromo via Matron, via me, to you. He wants to know if Elmer's still enjoying himself, and he hopes he isn't being any trouble."

"I should say he's enjoying himself like a house on fire," said Darbishire mournfully. "He's probably laughing himself black in the gills at this very moment."

"And he's not being any trouble?"

"Oh, no," replied Jennings in a faint, far-away sort of voice. "He's not being any trouble at all, thanks very much."

Jennings trudged slowly up the stairs, and from a landing window he caught sight of Mr. Carter and Mr. Wilkins on the tennis court, battling for the last point of a keenly-fought game. He stopped for a moment, and, as he watched, Mr. Wilkins slammed the ball hard into the net, and the game was over.

Masters had all the luck, Jennings decided. No troubles or worries, and nothing to do all evening except to enjoy themselves how and when they pleased. He sighed and passed on up the stairs.

Outside, on the tennis court, Mr. Carter replaced his racket in its press while Mr. Wilkins slackened the net.

"Phew!" Mr. Wilkins mopped his brow. "That last set was pretty strenuous. What about coming for a swim?"

"I'd rather cool off a bit first," replied Mr. Carter.

"It'll be dark before we finish if we don't go now; the dormitory bell went five minutes ago. Hind has just been whistling the boys back from the pond." Mr. Wilkins laughed. "Poor old Hind! I'll bet he'd rather come in for a nice cool dip with us, than traipse about on dormitory duty."

Mr. Carter was not quite sure that he wanted a nice cool dip, but he accompanied his colleague to the swimming bath all the same. When he saw the state of the water he *was* quite sure!

"No," he said firmly. "I'm not swimming in that. I'll wait until Robinson's changed the water."

"You shouldn't bother about a little grime on the surface," replied Mr. Wilkins genially, as he disappeared into a cubicle to change. "It does you good to have a swim every day. Takes your mind off Form 3."

"My mind doesn't need taking off Form 3."

"Well, mine does," came through the cubicle door. "That boy, Jennings, for instance. He was deliberately trying to

43

give me facetious answers all through the geometry lesson this afternoon."

Mr. Carter sat on a bench and filled his pipe. "I wouldn't be too sure they were *meant* to be facetious, Wilkins," he said. "They may have sounded funny to you, but that's because, at the age of ten, Jennings' mind doesn't work in quite the same way that yours does."

"Nonsense; you're making excuses for him," replied his colleague. "If I had my way I'd . . . I say, Carter, there's a glass tank in this cubicle. Where on earth has that come from?" But there seemed to be little point in pursuing the matter, while the swimming bath lay cool and tempting before him.

Mr. Wilkins was a strong swimmer, but an uncertain diver. He stood poised for a moment on the spring-board and then launched himself into the air. There was a sharp smack as he hit the water, and Mr. Carter hastily moved back as the wash billowed over and drenched the matting round the edge of the pool. Mr. Wilkins swam under water for a few strokes and then spluttered his way to the surface.

"Ah, that's better!" he called. "You should have come in, Carter; it's lovely in here."

"I'll take your word for it," replied Mr. Carter, eyeing the water with distaste. Vaguely he wondered how a film of biscuit crumbs—or was it sawdust?—came to be floating on the bath at all. In point of fact, it was powdered fish-food, but he had no means of knowing that.

"Well, as I was saying," Mr. Wilkins went on, rolling over on his back and churning the water noisily with both feet, "I warned Jennings that if I had any more funny answers from him, I should go off the deep end about it."

"What did you say?" Mr. Carter found it difficult to hear above the plash of his colleague's vigorous back-stroke.

"I said I'd go off the deep end."

"You've just done that," said Mr. Carter. "I felt the splash."

"No, what I meant was . . ." Mr. Wilkins broke off and roared with laughter. "Ha-ha-ha—That was jolly good!

44

I could make up a funny story out of that—Form 3 would love it. I'll tell them I was just going to dive and I thought about Jennings, so I went off the deep end. Ha-ha-ha . . ."

The mirth ended in a sudden gurgle as the swimmer's face disappeared beneath the surface. A second later, when he came to the top, his jocular mood had gone, for few people can indulge in hearty laughter under the water without serious discomfort.

"Ach! . . . Gll! . . . Pff! . . . Corwumph! " gasped Mr. Wilkins. "I say, Carter, this water's filthy."

"I can see that. We can't let the boys use it again until it's been properly cleaned out. I'll tell Robinson to start draining it, right away."

"And look at the muck in it," protested the swimmer. "Dash it, I got an earful of pondweed when I went under just now. That sort of stuff shouldn't be growing in an indoor swimming bath. And besides that . . . Good heavens! "

"What's the matter?"

A look of amazement passed across Mr. Wilkins' damp features. "I say, Carter," he gasped, "I'm seeing things. I—I've just seen a fish! "

"Nonsense," replied Mr. Carter. "This isn't an aquarium."

"No, but, dash it, I did see it; it shot right past me. Some sort of carp, it looked like. I've had enough of this —I'm coming out." And with swift strokes, Mr. Wilkins swam to the side and climbed from the water. He was gravely perturbed. Things had come to a pretty pass, he thought, when the school swimming bath sprouted pondweed and teemed with marine life.

"Impossible," Mr. Carter told him. "You imagined it."

"I tell you, I did see a fish," his colleague insisted. "It swam right past me snapping its jaws. It was as big as that, easily." He held out his hands to demonstrate the size; then, noting Mr. Carter's smile of disbelief, he reduced the dimensions to about a handsbreadth. "It must have been that big, anyway," he maintained.

"What a pity it got away! A specimen that size would

look most imposing if it were stuffed and put in a glass case," replied Mr. Carter, still wearing his amused smile.

Mr. Wilkins gave him a look. "You don't believe me, do you? You think I'm trying to be funny."

"No funnier than Jennings tries to be when he gives you an answer you didn't expect."

There was a puzzled frown on Mr. Wilkins' face all the time he was dressing. He couldn't have been mistaken about a thing like that; and yet . . . He gave it up. That sort of thing didn't happen in well-regulated preparatory schools!

As the masters were leaving the bath, they met Robinson, the odd-job man, on the door-step. He was known to the boys as Old Pyjams, for no better reason than that his opposite number, the night-watchman, was known as Old Nightie. It was no news to Robinson that the water needed changing, and indeed he had arrived for that very purpose. He always opened the sluice valve in the evening, he explained, so that the water would have all night in which to drain away, and the bath would be ready to be cleaned the following morning before it was re-filled.

"Does it take all night to empty?" asked Mr. Wilkins.

"Oh yes, sir; very slow to drain it is because of the filter. We had that fitted two years ago on account of the boys dropping things into the bath, accidental like, and losing them for good and all."

He was a young man, was "Old" Pyjams and always ready for a chat. "You'd be surprised at the things I find washed up against the filter sometimes when I clean the bath out," he went on. "Gym shoes, cricket balls, towels —all manner. Why, I found a wrist-watch on the bottom last summer; been there the best part of three weeks. Wasn't going, though," he finished sorrowfully.

When the masters had gone, Robinson opened the sluice valve and "tut-tutted" at the colour of the water, now draining slowly away. It was less than three weeks since he had re-filled the bath and he could hardly believe that seventy-nine boys could make so much water so dirty in so short a time. But then, he was not allowing for a tin full of fish food, an armful of pond-weed and a flower-pot full of earth.

At the first note of the rising bell, Jennings leapt out of bed and roused the sleeping Darbishire with an impatient jerk of the sheet. As a rule they rose in a leisurely manner and spent some time practising clove-hitches with their dressing-gown cords, but today urgent work lay ahead.

Venables, Atkinson and Temple, with whom they shared Dormitory 4, had only arrived at the yawning and head-scratching stage when Jennings and Darbishire hurried from the room.

Jennings went for the key while Darbishire fetched his butterfly-net from the games room.

"I've botched the hole up a bit," he said as they met outside the swimming bath, "but it's rather like locking the stable door after the horse has bolted."

Jennings inspected the repair work. "I should think the horse could still get through this net, the way you've mended it."

"Which horse?"

"The one you were talking about."

"Oh, but there isn't a horse, really!"

"You said there was."

"No, it's just a saying. I didn't mean it literally. We don't really want to catch a horse, do we?"

"Well, stop nattering about stable doors, then," said Jennings, as he fumbled with the lock and stepped over the threshold. "It ought to be pretty easy to catch him now the ground bait's had time to work, so all we've got to do is to lure him to the side, and I'll lean over and . . . Oh, gosh! . . . Oh, crumbs! . . . Darbishire, look!"

Darbishire *was* looking. Together they stood and stared at the empty swimming bath in dismay. Little pools lay in hollows all along the bottom and the flower-pot was floating against the strainer at the far end. But of Elmer there was no sign.

They climbed down to the floor of the bath and inspected each puddle with care, for some of the hollows were deep enough to afford temporary shelter for a three-inch fish. It was all to no purpose, and even a minute inspection of the filter failed to reveal any fish-like trace.

"This is ozard," moaned Darbishire. "He must have gone down the drain with the water. Gosh, what a frantic bish! Whatever will Bromo say?"

"Quite a lot, I expect," Jennings answered unhappily. "He may even have a relapse. After all, how would you feel if someone told you that your next-of-kin had gone down the plughole in the bath?"

"He wouldn't," Darbishire objected. "My father says that our bath at home is too small for him to lie down in properly, so he couldn't . . ."

"Well, you know what I mean. Now we must keep calm, Darbi, and think things out. If we can find where the water goes when it runs away, there's just a chance we might be able to find him. It's a million to one, I admit, but he may still be alive."

"Do you think so?" breathed Darbishire. "My father says that while there's life there's hope."

"Well, provided Elmer's got enough water, we can still go on hoping."

"That's right," Darbishire agreed. "All he needs is plenty of hope and water." He brightened a little and the numbed look faded from behind his spectacles. "Hope and water," he repeated. "Gosh, Jen, I could make up a creasingly funny pun about hope and water, if I set my mind to it."

Jennings turned to his friend and his expression was a mixture of anger and despair. "Dash it all, Darbi! " he protested. "This is no time to be making ridiculous Form 1 jokes. This is a matter of life and death! "

"Sorry, Jen," said Darbishire humbly, and followed his friend out of the swimming bath.

CHAPTER FIVE

The Kettle of Fish

DURING BREAKFAST, Jennings thought hard. He was more than willing to confess to his presence in the swimming-bath, if such a course would help to restore Elmer to his tank. But he felt that the staff would show little sympathy towards the fate of one small fish, and they would certainly forbid rescue operations if this meant interfering with school routine.

The best course, he decided, would be to find out what happened to the water when it flowed away. Until he had done so, it would be wiser to say nothing, for Bromwich was only just recovering from an attack of mumps, and one must never alarm an invalid in a delicate state of health.

After breakfast and during break, Jennings made a few guarded inquiries, and one of the gardeners told him all he needed to know. After passing through the filter, the water was carried underground by pipes until it emerged in a ditch near the pond. Then it flowed across a meadow which the boys seldom used, for this part of the school grounds was rented by a neighbouring farmer.

Wednesday was a half-holiday, and immediately after lunch, Jennings and Darbishire set out on their errand of mercy. Operation Rescue had replaced Operation Exercise and, as Jennings pointed out, this applied to Operation Geometry Exercise as well, for Elmer's recapture must certainly be attended to without delay.

They passed the pond and followed the ditch across the meadow, examining every foot of water as they went.

"This seems pretty hopeless to me," Jennings observed after nearly an hour's fruitless search. "We've come about a hundred miles already, and we haven't seen a whisker of him."

"Of course we haven't—they don't have whiskers," Darbishire corrected. "Now, if we were looking for a cat, you *could* say we hadn't seen a whisker."

"But we're not looking for a cat, you prehistoric remains! "

"No, but *supposing* we were."

Jennings, mudsplashed and miserable, turned on his companion with some heat. "What's the point of *supposing* we're looking for a cat, when you know jolly well we're looking for a fish? Come on, Darbi, we've got to follow this ditch till we get to the end of it—wherever that is."

"That'll be about another hundred miles, I expect," said Darbishire. He removed his spectacles and polished them with his tie. "Oh, gosh, isn't this a ghastly hoo-hah! There's just about everything else you can think of in this ditch—frogs and toads and newts and stinging nettles and old boots—everything except a goldfish."

They both knew in their heart of hearts that the quest was a failure, but neither of them would admit it. Darbishire replaced his glasses and his gaze wandered listlessly round the meadow. "Where have we got to?" he demanded. "I've never been here before. Aren't we out of bounds?"

"We're still on school property," Jennings told him, "only we don't come here because Farmer Arrowsmith uses it to graze his old cow in."

"Oh, I see," Darbishire replied. "That explains why . . . Oh! I say, Jen, I believe I can see it, now I've cleaned my glasses."

"Oh, wizzo! " shouted Jennings, his hopes rising like an express lift. "Quick, Darbi—where?"

"Over there, look! "

Jennings followed the line of the pointing finger to where a middle-aged cow seemed to be playing some form of basketball with a turnip. Patiently he explained the difference between a cow and goldfish.

"Oh, I didn't mean Elmer," Darbishire pointed out. "I meant I could see Farmer Arrowsmith's old cow. What do you think we ought to do? She's coming over here."

"Do? We needn't do anything. Cows don't hurt you."

"They do if they're bulls," said Darbishire uneasily. "And, anyway, I'm not very fond of cows, even if you're sure that's what it is. I've got a sort of feeling about them."

"You must be like my Aunt Angela. She has the same sort of feeling about cats. She hates them; she can always tell when there's a cat in the room."

"Well, I could always tell if there was a cow in the room," retorted Darbishire logically; and he sidled towards a tree whose branches offered shelter in case of attack.

"Don't be such a great funk, Darbi!" snorted Jennings contemptuously. "You don't want to be afraid of a harmless old . . ." He broke off and glanced at the cow with sudden misgiving. She had abandoned her basketball and was charging towards the boys as fast as her horny hoofs would permit.

Jennings stared: this cow was not friendly, perhaps she held strong views on the laws of tresspass; perhaps she felt as strongly about boys as Darbishire felt about cows; perhaps . . . He ceased his speculations and joined his friend in the lower branches of the tree.

The cow arrived at the tree and moo'ed at them from below. Then, as nothing happened, she thudded away to resume her game on the far side of the meadow.

The boys were tired of the ditch, so they sat for a while in the tree, discussing what to do next. It was clear that they were wasting their time, to say nothing of incurring further trouble; for Jennings should have been hard at work on his geometry exercise, and Darbishire should have been playing cricket. Finally, they decided that the music would have to be faced, and the news of his sad loss must be broken to Bromwich without delay. They would buy him another fish—two fishes, if he liked, plus any other form of compensation that he might demand. With the best of intentions, they had done Bromwich a great wrong, and they were prepared to stand with bowed heads while his wrath cascaded about their ears.

They felt a little better after this decision and were about to climb down from the tree, when they observed Mr. Wilkins crossing the meadow. "Oh, golly, we've had it now!" said Jennings. And he was right—they had!

"What on earth are you two boys doing up there?" Mr. Wilkins had the sort of voice that would be highly commended in any competition for town criers, and though he was still forty yards from the tree, there was no need for him to raise his voice above its normal volume. "You've no business to be in this part of the grounds at all," he went on, as the boys climbed down and stood guiltily before him. "You haven't finished that exercise yet, have you, Jennings?"

"No, sir, I haven't *quite* got to the end of it yet, sir."

"Why not?"

"Because—well, because I haven't quite got to the beginning part yet, sir."

"Exactly," boomed Mr. Wilkins. "Just as I thought. And you climbed up that tree hoping that I shouldn't see you!"

"Oh, no, sir, really," Darbishire assured him. "We thought we were going to be attacked by a fierce cow, but it was a mistake, and you turned up instead, sir." Even as he said it he knew that, as an excuse, it sounded rather feeble—especially as the cow was now out of sight.

Mr. Wilkins thought so, too. "Nonsense!" he said. "You were making a deliberate attempt to keep out of my way."

"Oh, but we weren't, sir, honestly. We never even saw you until you saw us," Jennings protested.

"No? Then do you mind telling me"—and Mr. Wilkins dropped his voice to a quiet, confident undertone—"do you mind telling me just what you *were* doing?"

"We—we were looking for a fish, sir."

"What! *Up a tree?*"

"Well, yes and no, sir. I mean . . ."

"I—I—Corwumph! I've had quite enough of this insolence," barked Mr. Wilkins, turning three shades pinker. "I warned you only yesterday what would happen if I had any more funny answers from you. You'll go straight back to school immediately, and report to me in the staff room."

"Yes, sir."

Mr. Wilkins strode away, furious at what he considered to be a facetious and impertinent answer to his question, and the two boys turned their footsteps towards home. It was not a cheerful journey and after they had walked a hundred yards in silence, Darbishire said: "You are a fool, Jen!"

"Well, it wasn't my fault," his friend defended himself. "We really *were* looking for a fish."

"Yes, but you put it badly. Even Old Wilkie knows fish don't live in trees, unless you're speaking alley—er, alley-something."

"Alibi?"

"No, allegorically, that's it: it means saying something that sounds quite crazy, but it's all right really, because everyone knows what you mean."

"Do they? That's more than *I* do!"

"Well, it's like that chunk of English we had to learn for Mr. Carter, about sermons in stones, and books in the running brooks."

"You're bats!" Jennings retorted. "There wouldn't be any books in the brook unless someone had put them there."

"That's exactly what I mean. There wouldn't be any fish up a tree either because they can't climb. At least," he went on, "if one *did* climb a tree it'd be all over the newspapers. Big headlines: *Goldfish's Amazing Feat!*"

"Yes, it would be, if it had any, wouldn't it?"

"Wouldn't it *what*?"

"It'd be amazing if a goldfish had got any feet."

Darbishire began to realise that they were talking at cross-purposes. Curtly he said: "No, you ancient relic, I didn't mean that sort of feet."

"For heaven's sake stop talking nonsense," Jennings answered. "There's no point in arguing about what sort of feet it's got, if it hasn't got any."

53

They were too tired of the subject to talk any more, and they finished the journey in gloomy silence. They met Atkinson as they were crossing the quad; he came bounding towards them with another message he had received from Bromwich, via Matron, via him, to Jennings. Elmer's next-of-kin, it seemed, was thirsting for the latest bulletin about his pet's welfare.

"Well, actually. we've made a bit of a bish over Elmer and we've lost him," Jennings admitted.

"Lost him!" Atkinson sounded incredulous. "Gosh, you must be absent-minded! Have you looked carefully all round his tank?"

"It's worst than that," said Jennings. "He's gone for good. Darbi's going up to Matron to ask her to see Bromo and break it to him gently."

They had no time to satisfy Atkinson's curiosity, for Jennings had an appointment with Mr. Wilkins which it would be unwise to overlook. But his main worry was about Bromwich: how on earth could he soften the blow? There seemed no answer to this problem and his heart was heavy as he knocked on the staff room door.

Mr. Carter was alone when Jennings opened the door and asked: "Sir, is Mr. Wilkins here, please, sir?"

It seemed rather a pointless question to Mr. Carter, for the staff room was sparsely furnished and the chances that his colleague was hiding behind the bookcase were remote. He pointed this out.

"Yes, I see, sir. We must have raced him back, then," said Jennings. "I'd better go and look for him, because I've got to report at once." He was about to close the door behind him, when Mr. Carter called him back.

"By the way, Jennings: when you find Mr. Wilkins will you tell him from me that swimming will have to be cancelled this afternoon. Robinson hasn't finished cleaning the bath out yet."

"Yes, sir." And in a burst of confidence the boy added: "It was rotten luck that the bath was emptied last night, sir."

54

"I don't agree," said Mr. Carter. "It was high time that water was changed. You probably won't believe it, but Robinson tells me that when he went there at half-past six this morning to see if the bath was empty, he found . . . I'll give you three guesses."

Jennings got it in one. "I know, sir; a goldfish!"

"Well, well," said Mr. Carter. "I might have known you'd had something to do with it. You'd better tell me what happened."

Jennings was thankful for the opportunity; his troubles had been preying heavily on his mind, and Mr. Carter was a very understanding sort of man. There was a punishment, of course—no swimming for a week for going to the bath without permission. But Jennings was glad about this, for if Bromwich was to suffer, it was only right that the culprits, too, should pay some penalty for their folly. Then he realised that Mr. Carter was still speaking, and what he was saying meant that Bromwich would not have to suffer after all.

". . . and if it hadn't been for the strainer, you'd have lost him altogether," Mr. Carter finished up.

"Do you mean the fish is all right then, sir?" Jennings gasped in wonder.

"Perfectly. It's as lively a fish as I ever saw. Robinson found it flapping about in a puddle near the strainer, and the only thing he could find to put it in was a kettle that the night watchman uses for his tea."

"Oh, sir—how supersonic, sir! Thanks awfully, sir! Gosh, this is the best news I've ever heard, sir! May I go and get him and put him back in his tank, please, sir?"

"The sooner the better," replied Mr. Carter. "Robinson's put the kettle in the woodshed for the time being. I said I'd let him know what to do with it, later on."

Outside in the corridor Darbishire was waiting. He had delivered the doleful news to Matron who had agreed to pass it on after tea, when her patient might be feeling strong enough to withstand the shock. After that, Darbishire went downstairs to wait for Jennings, and he was more than a little surprised when his friend shot out of the staff room wearing the sort of expression on his face that was not usually worn after unpleasant interviews with Mr. Wilkins.

"Did you find him, Jen?" he inquired.

"No, but I know where he is," Jennings called back gaily. "He's in a kettle in the woodshed."

"Who—Mr. Wilkins?"

"No—Elmer. Mr. Carter said they found him when they let the water out and he got stopped by the strainer."

"Who—Mr. Carter?"

"No, you ancient monument, I'm still talking about the fish."

"Oh, good!" cried Darbishire, as light dawned. "I thought your hoo-hah with Old Wilkie had been so ghastly that you'd gone stark raving bats and I should have to humour you."

The woodshed was on the far side of the kitchen yard at the rear of the main school buildings: the two boys dashed madly along the corridors and across the quad and never slackened pace until their goal was in sight. Speed was essential; not only because they were eager to see Elmer again, but also in case the night watchman should decide to make himself a cup of tea without first inspecting the kettle. Panting and breathless, the rescuers reached the woodshed and hastened inside.

Mr. Wilkins was a little late in arriving back at school, for he had met Farmer Arrowsmith and had been obliged to stop and listen to a short lecture on the state of British farming; but now he was anxious to deal with Jennings without further delay, so he took a short-cut across the kitchen garden in order to save time. As he picked his way across the cabbage patch, he caught sight of two figures disappearing through the door of the woodshed; one had dark brown hair, and the other was fair and curly. They were some distance away, but Mr. Wilkins had no difficulty in recognising them. After all, it was less than half an hour since he had seen them up a tree.

"I—I—Corwumph!" he muttered. He turned three

shades pinker and his mood was volcanic as he altered his course and strode towards the woodshed door.

It was dark inside the shed, and for a moment the boys could see nothing. There was a window, but it was covered with cobwebs; and so, too, was Darbishire by the time he had groped his way past the bundles of firewood piled high upon the floor. Jennings found the kettle in the darkest corner and hurried with it to the window.

"I've got it, Darbi. Hurray, Elmer's saved!" he cried in triumph.

"Wizzo!" shouted Darbishire through his cobwebs.

Jennings brushed the dirt from one of the panes with his fingers, and a little light streamed in and lit up the occupant of the kettle. "He's all right, too," Jennings went on. "He's swimming about like blinko. Come over here and have a look."

"I can't look," complained Darbishire. "I'm covered in cobweb. I walked straight into the blackest one I ever saw. Or rather, I didn't actually see it, or I shouldn't have walked into it; and now it's all over my face, I can't see anything at all."

"I can," said Jennings. "I can see . . ." He was going to say: "I can see Elmer doing his famous backwards breast-stroke," but a shadow passed across the window and the boy looked out to see who it was. "I can see Mr. Wilkins and I think he's coming in," he finished up, and his tone had lost much of its gaiety.

The door screeched open on its rusty hinges, and Mr. Wilkins burst in like the advance guard of an armoured column.

"Come here at once, you two boys," he boomed, and in the confines of the tiny shed his voice sounded as though the armoured column was making the most of its heavy artillery. "I told you to report to me in the staff room, Jennings."

"Yes, sir, I did, sir, but you weren't there, sir. I was going to come and look for you, sir, but . . ."

"You didn't think you'd find me in the woodshed, did you?"

"Oh no, sir, but . . ."

"But you thought it would be a good place to hide in," Mr. Wilkins broke in. "Trying to evade me, eh? So that's the nigger in the woodpile, is it!"

"No, sir, that's Darbishire," Jennings explained. "He only looks like that because he's got a bit cobwebby, and we weren't hiding from you, honestly, sir."

"Then what on earth *are* you doing in here?"

"We're—we were looking for a kettle of fish, sir."

It was an unfortunate way to describe it and, as Darbishire remarked afterwards, talking about kettles of fish put the lid on it.

"I—I—Corwumph! I've had enough of these insolent answers. Gross impudence and rank impertinence! You'll come along with me to the Headmaster's study immediately."

Mr. Wilkins led the way out into the sunlight and the boys followed him. Darbishire made an attempt to tidy himself, but he merely succeeded in smearing the cobwebs over the cleaner parts of his neck and ears. He removed his spectacles and wiped the dust from the lenses with his even dustier fingers.

"We'll see what the Head has to say about deliberate attempts to be funny," said Mr. Wilkins. "And what's more, I gave you fair warning about . . ." He stopped abruptly, for he had just noticed that Jennings was carrying an unusual object. "What have you got there?" the master demanded.

"It's the kettle of fish, sir," Jennings replied. "I told you there was one and you wouldn't believe me. Look, sir, you can see the fish swimming about inside."

Mr. Wilkins stared. "I—I—well, I—Corwumph!" he said. It was not a very profound remark, but for the moment he could think of nothing else to say.

They did not go to the Headmaster's study. They went, instead, to the staff room, where Mr. Carter filled in the gaps in the story for the benefit of his colleague. Mr. Wilkins was still very annoyed, but he was a fair-minded man, and when he realised that Jennings' answers had been made in good faith, and that the boys had had permission to visit the woodshed, he took a more tolerant view of their activities. They had already been punished for misusing the swimming baths, so apart from a few curt comments about geometry exercises, there was little more to be said.

"You can go now," said Mr. Wilkins when he had exhausted his stock of curt comments. "Go and start that geometry exercise at once."

"Yes, sir. Thank you, sir. Will it be all right if I put the fish back in his tank first, sir, and then tell Matron that she needn't break it gently after all, sir?"

"What on earth should Matron want to break it for? Look here, if you're starting . . ."

"Oh, no, sir," Jennings explained hastily. "I don't mean break the tank—I meant the news. She won't have to tell Bromwich that his next-of-kin has slipped down the plug-hole after all, sir."

As the door shut behind the two boys, Mr. Wilkins turned to his colleague with a puzzled frown.

"Next-of-kin?" he echoed. "What on earth's the silly little boy drivelling about, Carter? The trouble with Jennings is that he lets his imagination run away with him. Fish nesting in trees and lurking in kettles—he needs bringing down to earth. I've a good mind to make him write out 'I must not let my imagination run away with me' a hundred times."

Mr. Carter rose from his chair and knocked his pipe out in the fireplace. "I don't think I should do that, Wilkins," he said. "We all do the same thing at times, even though we're not ten-year-olds."

"Nonsense," replied Mr. Wilkins. "I've got my imagination under control all right!"

"I wonder! You remember that fish that frightened you out of the swimming bath, yesterday evening? A large carp, I believe, that snapped its jaws at you."

Mr. Wilkins could see where the conversation was leading. "I—I—well, what of it?" he demanded.

"I was only thinking," Mr. Carter went on, "that as it's the same one that you saw just now in that little kettle, it's either shrunk during the night, or you let your imagination run away with you yesterday, when you told me how big it was."

"I—er, h'm," said Mr. Wilkins thoughtfully.

"So I don't think that a hundred lines for Jennings would be quite fair in this case, do you?"

Mr. Wilkins frowned hard at the waste-paper basket for some moments. Then he said slowly: "Perhaps you're right, Carter . . . Perhaps you're right."

CHAPTER SIX

Maiden Voyage

THE LITTLE HUT was finished. The bulrush curtains flapped gaily over the unglazed window; the painting of the green-faced cow stared moodily from its picture-frame; on the threshold, the doormat welcomed visitors to *Ye Oldë Worldë Huttë* in letters of coloured bottle-tops.

Some of the more ambitious ideas had been reluctantly abandoned. The Headmaster had refused to allow camp cookery on open fires even though the patent fire-extinguisher stood ready to hand; the refrigerator was not a success either, and the ageing pork pie had long since been thrown into the pond; but as the living-room was becoming rather full of gadgets, the extra space was more than welcome.

There was nothing else to do now, except to enjoy the fruits of their labour, so Jennings invited Temple and Venables to a hut-warming party. They squatted on the floor—no longer wet, thanks to the special dehydrating canal—and ate walnut cake and sardines, which they washed down with a tin of condensed milk.

"Now it's all finished," Jennings told his guests, "we're going to take up some interesting hobbies with the hut as our headquarters. We can't just sit inside all the time, like a couple of spare dinners, and look at the furniture.

"We *were* going to collect tadpoles," added Darbishire, hacking two holes in the condensed milk tin with his pen-knife, "but after that hoo-hah about Elmer we both felt a little 'off' fish." His penknife penetrated the lid with a sudden gurgle, forcing little bubbles of milk through the outlet hole on the other side.

"Aerial bombardment would be a super-cracking hobby," suggested Venables. "We could climb up trees and try and score direct hits on other chaps' huts with hunks of turf."

"No fear," said Jennings firmly. "We've been to a lot of trouble to build decent shacks, so what's the point of knocking them down? Besides, our hut is a supersonic sight too near a tree—we'd be the first one to suffer the bomb damage."

Darbishire nodded in agreement and said: "That's quite right. It's like what my father says about people who live in glass houses not throwing stones, or rather, people who live in reed huts shouldn't bung turf—it's the same thing, really."

"It's not the same thing at all," objected Temple with his mouth full of cake and sardine. "If you can't tell the diff. between a glass house and an igloo . . ."

"You don't understand. It's just a saying," Darbishire pointed out. "There are no such things as glass houses, really."

"There wizard well are! " Temple maintained. "We've got one at home. We grow tomatoes in it, so that proves it."

"Yes, I know, but I meant the other sort."

"What other sort?"

"The sort that if you live in them, you shouldn't throw stones."

"But a moment ago, you said there *was* no other sort. You told us there was no such thing."

"Yes, but I meant . . . Oh, never mind. Have a drink! " And Darbishire licked his sticky fingers, and thrust the condensed milk at his guest.

Venables was forced to admit that aerial bombardment sounded rather feeble when compared with the idea which suddenly sprang up in Jennings' mind. "Let's make a model yacht," he suggested.

They seized upon his idea eagerly. The setting was perfect—a reed-fringed pond was just the place for hobbies with a nautical flavour. In a flash their minds leapt into the future, foreseeing squadrons of model yachts in full sail, skimming gracefully across the little muddy pond. They felt the thrill of the neck-and-neck finish in the famous four-lengths handicap race; they saw the annual regatta attended by craft which ranged from *F* class models down to odd bits of cigar-box with penholder masts. The possibilities of a yacht club were endless; they could build a club house with *Members Only* inscribed on the door; officers would be elected—presidents, secretaries, commodores and admirals who would be entitled to strut about wearing yachting caps.

In a few minutes they had formed a committee and were hard at work drafting the rules. Darbishire was appointed secretary and filled three pages of his notebook with the Minutes of the meeting. Then he read them out.

"*Rule One*. Any character wanting to join the club must have a boat that actually floats. *Rule Two . . .*"

"Hang on a sec," objected Temple. "We're putting the cart before the horse. We haven't got a boat between us yet, so we can't even be members, let alone commodores and things."

It was, without doubt, a serious drawback, and Jennings descended to brass tacks right away. "We'll have to get cracking and make one then," he said. "We can't have a model yacht club until we've got a model yacht."

They cancelled the committee meeting and set to work. Temple and Venables scavenged for suitable pieces of wood while Jennings went off to borrow a chisel from the carpenter's shop. Darbishire retired to his small back room, armed with his notebook, to design the stately lines on which the boat was to be built. If only he had brought his geometry box with him, he could have constructed his blue-print with more accuracy; but no one takes geometrical instruments to a hut-warming party, so he did the best he could with a stub of pencil, using a damp forefinger as a rubber.

The yacht was not built that day. It took two days to collect the materials, and a further three evenings' hard work was necessary before the craft could be described as remotely ship-shape. When at last it was finished, the four boys stood round in wide-eyed admiration!

"Isn't she rare," breathed Venables. "And she'll be sailing in uncharted waters too, because no one knows how deep the pond is in the middle."

"We'll soon find that out if she capsizes on her maiden voyage. If the mast's still showing above water when she's on the bottom, it can't be more than a foot deep," Temple argued.

The design of the boat had little in common with the usual type of yacht, for it was shaped rather like a flat-bottomed barge. It was three feet long: the hull was weighted with a small brick so that it would not ride too high in the water and, as a precaution, Darbishire's sponge had been built into the fo'c's'l, in case the vessel should not ride high enough. The sail had caused some trouble, for the school sewing room had turned out to be a disappointing marine store when Jennings went there in search of sail-cloth. In the end he decided to rig his handkerchief into a single square sail, as favoured by the Vikings. Experts would have been critical of the craft's ungainly lines, but the boys had made the whole thing themselves and they prized it above any factory-built model.

"Not bad is she!" cooed Darbishire. "Your handkerchief makes a supersonic sail, Jen."

And Venables added: "Quite out of the ordinary, too. You don't often see a pale black sail with blotches of red ink on it."

"My handkerchief is *not* pale black," Jennings defended himself. "It's just a rather dark white."

"Let's go and launch her now. I can hardly wait to see her skimming across the pond." Darbishire skipped up and down excitedly until he bumped his head on the hut's low ceiling and skipped no more.

"I vote we have a proper launching ceremony and crack a bottle of ginger pop against the bows," suggested Temple.

"We haven't got any ginger pop," said Venables.

"Well, a tin of condensed milk, then."

"Gosh, no!" Jennings was horrified. "The bows might bust before the tin, and then she'd founder in six fathoms of pond-weed and I shouldn't get my handkerchief back. It's a bit chronic, having to sniff all the time, as it is."

They carried the boat to the water's edge, but unfortunately the whistle blew before they had time to begin the launching ceremony. They "tut-tutted" with exasperation.

"That means waiting till tomorrow evening. I'll never be able to hold out all that long," complained Temple.

"Tomorrow's Sunday," Darbishire reminded him, "and we're not allowed over here in our best suits, so we'll have to wait now till next week."

They could not bring themselves to face a forty-eight hours' delay. It was too disappointing after so many days of patient toil.

"There's only one thing for it," said Jennings: "we'll have to fox over here tomorrow afternoon and have a go then."

The little group glanced at one another doubtfully. Sunday afternoon spelt Walk during term time, and there was no way of avoiding it. Unless of course . . . Four minds reached the same answer and the expression on four faces plainly said they were all agreed.

"Right-o, we'll do that, then," said Jennings.

The Sunday walk at Linbury was not, except for the youngest boys, the dismal crocodile procession which wanders forth from so many school gates on Sunday afternoons. Linbury Court was on the South Downs, not far from the sea. There was a village half a mile away, and the small town of Dunhambury lay some five miles to the west. It was ideal country for walks for there was little traffic except on the main road which ran past the school gates.

The usual practice was for boys to give their names to the master on duty and then set off in small groups to walk as far as the sea and back. They could vary this if they wished and follow the footpaths across the open downland, but always they had to inform the duty master of their route and report to him when they returned at four o'clock.

If, however, some pressing engagement awaited their return to school—the launching of a model yacht, for example—then it was possible for the walk to be shortened. Not officially, of course, and never when Mr. Carter was on duty, but the thing *could* be done if one was prepared to take the risk.

Mr. Wilkins was the master on duty that Sunday: he sat in the staff room after lunch and jotted down the names of the boys as they reported to him. Presently four third-formers approached in a body. "Please, sir, will you put us down, sir?"

Mr. Wilkins did so. "Jennings—Darbishire—Venables—Temple," he wrote, and looking up he inquired: "Are you going down to the sea?"

"Well, sir, *towards* the sea, sir," said Jennings, and left it at that.

And towards the sea they went. But after covering three hundred yards they swung round in a circle and arrived back at the far end of the school grounds near the pond. Cautiously they crept to the hut and carried the yacht down to the water's edge, but soon they stopped bothering about caution. No one was about, no one would disturb them: provided that they reported to Mr. Wilkins at four o'clock, all would be well. Or so they thought!

"We ought to name this ship," Darbishire said. "What about the H.M.S. *J. C. T. Jennings the First*? That's only fair, really, because it was all Jen's super-cracking wheeze in the first place."

"That's too many initials," replied the inventor of the super-cracking wheeze modestly. "I vote we call it the *Revenge* after Sir Richard Grenville."

"Coo, yes, that's wizzo: and this bunch of bulrushes can be Florés in the Azores where Sir Richard Grenville lay," cried Darbishire with enthusiasm.

They had recently studied Tennyson's *Revenge* in class with Mr. Carter and the poem had made a deep impression

66

on Darbishire. He stood on the bank and declaimed dramatically:

> " 'At Florés in the Azores, Sir Richard Grenville lay,
> And a pinnace, like a fluttered bird, came flying from
>   far away:
> Spanish ships of war at sea,
> We have sighted fifty-three . . .'

"Those two old moorhens over there can be the fifty-three . . .

> " 'Then sware Lord Thomas Howard . . .' "

The other members of the yacht club grew restive, for they were anxious to get on with the launching ceremony. "We can't wait for you to finish the whole poem, Darbi," they reminded him, and gathered round to watch the *Revenge* set sail on her maiden voyage.

"There she goes . . . Pheew-doyng! " said Jennings as the craft slid down the muddy slipway and hit the water with a splash.

For a moment they panicked as the boat rocked from side to side, but a moment later she righted herself, and they breathed again and gave three cheers. Whispered cheers, though, for they had no wish to draw undue attention to themselves.

There was a slight breeze which caught the "pale black" sail and the *Revenge* veered out to the middle of the pond while the boat-builders danced hornpipes of delight. Two moorhens were enjoying a peaceful Sunday afternoon swim, but when they saw the strange craft bearing down upon them they made for the bank at top speed.

"Look! " cried Darbishire. "The Spanish galleons are in retreat at full steam ahead. The *Revenge* will go *slap-bang-doyng* into them, if they don't look out! "

"She won't," replied Venables. "She'll go *doyng* into those reeds on the far side. Then what are we going to do?"

"I'll hoof round to the other side and head her off." Jennings was in charge and gave the orders.

"Stand by for Operation Salvage!" he cried, and ran as fast as he could round the rim of the pond.

Darbishire climbed up a small tree where he could obtain a better view. "It's a wonderful sight from here," he announced. "Just like Sir Richard Grenville." Odd snatches of the poem raced through his mind in a tangled disorder of lines.

" 'The little *Revenge* ran on sheer into the heart of the foe,
With her hundred fighters on deck, and her ninety sick below',"

he recited.

" 'Shall we fight or shall we fly?
Good Sir Richard tell us now,
For to fight is but to die!
There'll be little of us left by the time . . .'

"Yes, and there'll be little of our yacht left if she gets caught in those reeds," Temple pointed out. "She's heading straight for them at forty knots!" And a moment later his warning proved true and the *Revenge* stuck fast in the bulrushes.

By this time Jennings had reached the spot, but he was unable to reach out far enough to free the boat from its entanglements, for the reeds grew outwards from the bank and across the pond. There was only one thing to be done; a willow-tree grew on the bank and drooped its slender branches into the water. Jennings looked at it thoughtfully. If the branch would hold, he could crawl along until he was immediately above the *Revenge* and poke it back into clear water with a stick. The branch seemed fairly strong: he decided to try it.

On the far bank, Temple and Venables watched the salvage work with some anxiety.

"Looks massive perilous, doesn't it, Bod? I bet it won't hold him."

"It might, if he doesn't go too far, but he'll have to get nearly to the end before he can hoik it with that stick."

"Wow, it's quivering like an aspirin! Hadn't we better stand by with that inner tube in case he falls in?"

"He won't, if he's careful; and anyway, it's aspens that quiver, not aspirins."

"I bet you it's not. Besides, if that tree's a willow, it can't quiver like an aspen, so that proves it!"

"That's got nothing to do with it. It could be a Christmas tree for that matter—he'll still fall in if it won't hold him."

Darbishire looked down upon the discussion group with an air of detachment and wondered why they were making such a fuss. After all, *his* tree was quite safe and well away from the edge, and in his imagination he was sailing the Spanish Main with the more daring of the Elizabethan seamen. Would Sir Richard Grenville bother about getting his best suit wet? Would Sir Frances Drake turn back because the water was muddy? Darbishire stood up in his tree and encouraged the salvage work with lines of stirring poetry:

" 'We have won great glory, my men!
And a day less or more
At sea or ashore
We die—does it matter when?
Sink me the ship, Master Gunner—sink her, split her
    in twain!
Fall into the . . .' "

"Look out, Jen! " yelled Venables and Temple in unison, but the warning was too late. On the far side of the pond, Jennings felt the pliable branch sagging beneath his weight; it did not break, but, like the willow trees on *Linden Lea*, it bowed down low and gently tipped its burden head-over-heels into the water.

"Gosh, he *has* fallen in, too," Darbishire gasped in

horror. "I didn't mean fall into the pond, I meant fall into the . . ."

"Phew! There'll be a hoo-hah about this," breathed Venables, as Jennings rose to his feet, grabbed the *Revenge* and splashed damply up the bank.

Darbishire jumped down from his tree and rushed round to help his friend to safety. "Golly, Jen, you *are in* a mess! Are you all right?"

"Yes, *I* am," Jennings replied, "but my best suit isn't. I'm soaked to the skin."

They looked at the suit with horrified eyes. A black, fertile silt traced a pattern from shoulder to knees; little rivulets of muddy water trickled into the pockets, and pond-weed peeped shyly through the buttonholes.

"What a frantic bish! Why do these hoo-hahs always pick on *us* to happen to?" Darbishire wanted to know. "What are we going to do? You can't go back to school looking like Old Father Thames—Matron would be livid! That suit's nearly new, isn't it?"

Jennings nodded unhappily and wiped his face with the sail of the *Revenge*; it was the only portion of his clothing which was still dry. "This is ozard! " he lamented. "It's just trickling down me like the Niagara Falls! " He was worried, not merely on his own account, but because the disaster threatened the welfare of the whole colony of hut dwellers. Mr. Carter had warned them to avoid spoiling their clothes, and if this breach of rules ever became "front-page news" their activities in the area of the pond would come to an end.

There was only one way for the tragedy to be kept secret, and Jennings gave his orders as clearly as he could through teeth which were now beginning to chatter with cold. Venables and Temple were to hurry back to school and slip unnoticed into the dormitory; there they would find Jennings' week-day clothes which they were to bring back to the hut without delay.

"I shall want everything except a handkerchief," he told them. "You'll find them in my locker. Oh, yes, and bring a towel, too. Then, when I've changed, I'll fox down to the boiler-room and dry these wet things on the pipes. Go on, get cracking—I'm shivering like a brace of jellies already! "

"Come on, Bod," said Venables. "We'll have to be jolly careful we don't meet Old Wilkie on the way; and we'd better be pretty stealthy smuggling the stuff past Matron's room—she's got ears like a hawk."

"What about Darbi; isn't he coming with us?" asked Temple.

"No, he can stay and help keep the wind off me." And Jennings gave Temple an encouraging push to start him on his way. "Go on, get moving; I don't want to hang about here all day."

The relief party set off on its errand and Jennings squelched muddily back to the little hut. Darbishire followed carrying the *Revenge*. "Try not to leave dirty footmarks on the *Welcome* mat," he advised, but Jennings was past caring. The afternoon which had promised so well was petering out into a damp and chilly anti-climax. He sat back against the ventilating-shaft and shivered.

"Golly, you *are* in a bad way," Darbishire sympathised. "Can't you stop your teeth chattering?"

Jennings turned on him angrily. "Of course, I can't! You have a bash at stopping them if you're so clever."

"All right, keep cool! "

"I *am* keeping cool. An ozard sight too cool for my liking."

"Never mind, Jen! The *Revenge* put the fifty-three Spanish galleons to flight, anyway. You ought to have seen those moorhens wobbling back to base! " Darbishire prattled on in an attempt to make his friend more cheerful. "It's all rather like the poem, in a way—us two being left all alone after the others have gone. Remember that bit where it says:

" 'And the sun went down, and the stars came out . . .' ?"

"If you think I'm going to stay here shivering till the sun goes down . . ."

71

"No, but we can pretend you're one of the sick men down in the hold, who were most of them stark and cold."

"Huh! " Jennings' tone was crushing. "I don't have to do much pretending about that. I can feel frostbite setting in already."

Darbishire sighed as he carried the boat into the small back room. Until that wretched accident he had been quite carried away by the thrill of watching the *Revenge* riding the ripples on her maiden voyage; but now, all the poetry and glamour of the high seas seemed, somehow, to have faded, and nothing was left but a flat-bottomed barge, with a piece of sponge rammed into the fo'c's'l.

CHAPTER SEVEN

The Best Laid Plans . . .

THERE IS something unusual about the stillness which
descends upon preparatory schools on fine Sunday afternoons. Rooms which resound all day with shrill chatter,
and corridors which throb with noisy feet become strange,
unreal places when the building is deserted. By contrast,
the silence seems twice as deep, and sounds which are seldom heard catch the ear with twice the expected volume.
The ticking of a classroom clock, the rustling papers on
the notice board beside an open window, the fly buzzing
on the changing-room ceiling; these are the noises which
go on all day long—the little lost murmurs which are
swallowed up by the main stream of sound so that no one
is ever aware of them.

Temple and Venables sensed something of this quietness
as they crept through a side door into the empty hall. They
had met no one on their journey from the pond, though
they had taken special care when passing the Headmaster's
garden and again as they crossed the quad. So far, all was
well; none of the other boys had yet returned from their
afternoon walk and there was no sign of the master on
duty.

They pattered up the stairs, passing Matron's room on
tip-toe; then on, and up the next flight to Dormitory 4.

"This is working out more easily than I thought," remarked Venables as he opened the locker marked *J. C. T.
Jennings*. "There's nothing to go wrong now. All we've
got to do is to grab this little lot and beetle back to the
hut."

Everything was neatly laid out; suit, clean shirt, underwear, belt and socks. There was a pullover too, and though these were not worn during July, Venables added it to his collection in case of need. He bundled the garments together and shut the locker. "I'll carry these," he said. "You nip out on to the landing, Bod, and see if the coast's still clear."

"Right-o!" The whole thing had been so easy that Temple wore a smile on his lips and hummed gaily as he sauntered on to the landing. The next moment he was back; the humming had ceased and a worried frown had replaced the smile.

"It's no go, Ven," he whispered. "We're caught like rats in a trap!"

"Uh! What's happened?"

"Matron and Mr. Carter. They've just come out of Matron's sitting-room and they're nattering away like blinko on the landing outside her door. We should never be able to walk past them carrying all this clutter—they'd spot it in a flash."

"Oh, gosh, this *has* bished it up!" Venables sat on his bed, and his gaze roamed round the room in search of inspiration. What on earth could they do? Could they smuggle the clothes downstairs in that laundry basket, he wondered? But Temple poured cold water on the scheme when his friend suggested it. People who spot things in a flash could spot them in anything, he pointed out. "Dash it all, Venables, they know jolly well we aren't the dormitory maids, and if we go staggering down the stairs with a massive great wicker-work hamper in tow, they're bound to think it funny. We'll just have to wait till they hoof off."

They waited five minutes and again Temple crept out on to the landing. He returned shaking his head glumly. "They're still there. Can't think what they can find to go on talking about, hour after hour like that. You'd think grown-ups would have something better to do, wouldn't you?"

It was Venables who made the first practical suggestion. He suddenly smote himself on the brow as befitted a genius in the throes of a brainwave and said: "I've got it! We'll drop them out of the window and they'll go *doyng* down on to the quad. Then we can stroll downstairs past Matron and Mr. Carter, beef round to the quad and pick them up."

Nothing could have sounded simpler. They performed a short dance to show how pleased they were with the idea and then Temple skipped over to the window, flung it open and looked out.

"Stand out of the daylight, Bod; I'm going to bung," announced Venables. "One . . . two . . . three . . ." But with a sudden gasp of alarm, Temple withdrew his head and laid a restraining hand on his friend's arm. "Whoa, halt, stop! For Pete's sake, don't bung. Gosh, we nearly made a bish that time! " As he shut the window, he wiped imaginary beads of perspiration from his brow and his knees sagged with feigned weakness.

"What's wrong now?" demanded Venables, whose view was blocked by the bundle of clothes.

"Old Wilkie and the Head are standing just below the window. Phew, that was a chronic near squeeze! You'd have scored a direct hit on the Archbeako if I hadn't slammed the bomb doors in the nick of time."

They stood and looked at each other in blank despair. There was no way out; barriers sprang up at every turn. Surely no smuggler had ever had to face such difficulties.

"We've got to do something," said Venables five minutes later, after a furtive reconnaissance had shown that both the escape routes were still guarded. "We can't leave poor old Jen shivering his timbers and dripping like a tap, much longer."

"All taps don't drip; it's only when they need a new washer or something," Temple murmured vaguely.

"Don't quibble, Bod. We're not arguing about whether Jennings needs a new washer. What he *does* need are these dry clothes and somehow we've got to get them downstairs past Matron's observation turret. Why don't you try and think of something, instead of just sitting there and being feeble! "

"Well, I suppose we could, er—um . . ." Temple's mind

75

was a blank and he spoke for the sake of speaking, but even as he fumbled with the problem the answer flashed into his mind. "I know!" he finished up brightly. "You could put Jennings' clothes on underneath your own. Matron will never notice. She'll just think you've been putting on a bit of weight lately."

Venables stared at his friend in open-mouthed admiration. Here was a plan as ingenious as it was simple. This time, nothing *could* go wrong. Venables wasted no time; his own suit was off in a matter of seconds and he was scrambling into Jennings' underwear, shirt and socks. He dressed hurriedly; two pairs of shorts, one pullover and two jackets, and Venables stood ready to descend the stairs.

"Wizzo!" said Temple delightedly. "No one'll ever spot it. Don't leave that spare belt dangling—it'll give the show away. How does it feel?"

"It's a bit warm," Venables admitted, "and a bit cluttered up round the shoulders; I'll have to walk without swinging my arms or I shall bust out at the seams. How do I look?" One hand on hip, he minced along the dormitory in imitation of a mannequin at a dress parade.

"You look super," Temple encouraged him. "I should never have known you were wearing two lots; old Jen's suit fits you down to the ground."

"It hasn't got to do that. Down to the knees is quite far enough for short trousers. Now, what else is there? Oh, yes, shoes and a towel."

The towel was wrapped round Venables' chest between the outer layer of shirt and the pullover. The jacket buttons strained at their threads but he dared not leave them unfastened in case anyone should see what lay beneath.

"We'd better go downstairs one at a time," suggested Temple.

"Well, of course, you crumbling ruin. If I start leaping the stairs three at a time, it's just asking for Matron to sit up and take notice."

"No, I didn't mean that. I meant I'll go on ahead and get Jen's shoes from the bootlockers and wait for you by the side door. Don't forget to speed up a bit going past Mr.

Carter." Casually, Temple strolled out of the dormitory and sauntered down the stairs.

Matron and Mr. Carter were still on the lower landing discussing ways of improving the weekly shoe inspection. It was Matron's first term at Linbury; she was young and friendly and had a deep understanding of a boy's needs. They all liked Matron for she was a welcome change after her brisk and businesslike predecessor who had had little sympathy with junk-filled pockets and hair which would not stay parted. All the same, no Matron could be expected to take a tolerant view of best suits covered in fertile silt from the bottom of a pond.

Mr. Carter looked up as Temple came down the stairs. "You're back early, Temple. Did you go down to the sea?"

"We went part of the way, sir, and then we came back because—well, because we thought we'd come back," Temple finished lamely and hurried down to the boot-lockers.

A minute later, footsteps sounded again on the landing above and Venables, portly and self-conscious, walked down the stairs. He moved stiffly and his eyes stared straight ahead. He was just disappearing down the lower flight when Matron called him back.

"Oh, Venables, you're just the boy I want. I've got your new blazer; they sent it along from the tailor's yesterday and I want to see if it fits. Come into my sitting-room and try it on."

Venables rocked on his heels and clutched the banisters for support: "What—now, Matron?" he gulped.

"Yes, it won't take a minute."

"Oh, but, Matron, I . . ." He sought desperately for some excuse. "Couldn't I try it on after tea?"

"I shan't have time, then," Matron replied. "Come along, there's a good boy."

Numbly, he followed her into the sitting-room, while Mr. Carter, who was seldom deceived by anything, came in after him and closed the door.

"Here we are," said Matron, taking a magenta-and-white blazer from its box. "Slip your jacket off."

77

"My jacket! Oh, but, Matron, I . . . I can't!" He clutched the garment tightly about his chest and a lost and helpless look glazed his eyes. But he could not stand like that for ever and at last, very unwillingly, he unbuttoned his jacket, revealing a similar one underneath.

"Good gracious, what's the idea; you're not cold, are you?" Matron asked.

"He shouldn't be," said Mr. Carter, making a closer inspection. "He's got a pullover, a towel and two shirts on as well." He investigated further. "H'm! Two pairs of trousers, with a tangled assortment of braces . . . two pairs of socks . . . Are you going on an expedition to the South Pole by any chance, Venables?"

"No, sir. Not the South Pole, sir."

"But you're going on an expedition somewhere, aren't you?"

"Yes, sir. You see, what happened, sir . . ."

"I think I can guess." Mr. Carter glanced at the name-tape on the under-jacket. "Jennings has fallen into the pond. Right?"

"Yes, sir. Right in, sir."

"Oh, poor boy!" said Matron in a tone of such understanding that Venables gained a new respect for school matrons. "He'll catch his death of cold, hanging about in wet things. He'll have to have a hot bath at once."

"I'll go and fetch him. Take his clothes off, Venables, and wait here till I come back." At the door, Mr. Carter turned and said: "You know, Venables, you really are the *stupidest* little boy. Why on earth you couldn't say what had happened at the start instead of playing these ridiculous dressing-up games . . . !" He heaved a deep sigh and strode on to the landing and down the stairs.

It was some time before Jennings realised that the relief party must have met with an accident of some sort. The sun had gone in and his clothes were sticking to him in damp, uncomfortable patches.

"Come on, Darbi, let's go back," he suggested. "We've been here simply hours and hours—well, twenty minutes anyway and still nothing's happened. They've had time to make me a suit and knit me two pairs of socks by now."

"But you can't go back like that!"

"It'll be all right if I'm careful. We'll fox up to the dorm and I'll change into my every-day clothes while you take my wet ones down to the boiler-room."

"It's a bit risky," Darbishire demurred, but he knew that action of some sort was essential. He glanced at his watch; it was later than he thought and at four o'clock everyone had to report to the master on duty. This was a strict rule and there could be no evasion.

He rose to his feet. "If only Venables and Bod hadn't failed us in our hour of need! I suppose they've just beetled off with a light laugh and left us to it. My father says that a friend in need is a . . ."

"Come on, let's go!" Jennings crawled out of the hut and the two boys set off for the school buildings. Darbishire edged his way gingerly across the suspension bridge, but Jennings had no need for such refinements. He could not get any wetter, so he strode through the quagmire, mumbling threats.

"Wait till I see those two again! Leaving me to catch frostbite and chilblains and things—it's an ozard caddish trick!"

"Yes, I know. Sir Richard Grenville didn't just abandon his casualties like that," Darbishire replied as he rejoined his friend on dry land. "The *Revenge* ran sheer into the heart of the foe with ninety sick below, so that proves . . ."

"It must be nearly that now; it's cold enough," said Jennings through chattering teeth.

"It must be nearly *what*?"

"Ninety-six below freezing."

"I didn't say ninety-six *degrees*, you ancient relic; I said, 'Ninety comma, sick men'."

"You mean *coma*, not comma," Jennings retorted. "It's a sort of thing you go off into, if you're feeling as sick as I am. And Old Wilkie will be going off into one, if we don't report to him by four o'clock."

They left the wood and ran towards the cricket pitches;

luck was on their side to start with for the grounds seemed deserted, but as they were passing the hedge which bordered the Headmaster's garden, Jennings clutched his companion by the sleeve and dragged him into cover. "Ssh! There's someone coming!"

"Who?"

"I don't know, but I think it's a master. Quick, let's get through here."

Jennings knelt down and crawled through a gap in the hedge; Darbishire followed, considerably shaken. "But we're not allowed in here," he protested. "It's the Archbeako's garden. He attacks at zero feet with all his ammo blazing, if he finds anyone in here."

"We'll have to risk it, that's all."

They advanced a short distance into the garden and crouched behind a cucumber frame, while the footsteps drew near and passed by on the other side of the hedge. It was Mr. Carter, and he was heading for the pond.

When the master had gone, they crawled back on to the path and Darbishire breathed a sigh of relief. "Phew, that was a bit close! He didn't see us, though . . . I wonder where he's going?"

"Oh, nowhere special; he often beetles about. Good job we left the hut when we did, or he might have found us there and I shouldn't like him to know I'd got into this mess."

The boarders were returning from their walks when Jennings and Darbishire rounded the corner by the swimming bath, and Mr. Wilkins was on the quadrangle checking the names on his list as the boys reported to him. Clearly, it was impossible to gain the dormitory from this direction, so the two boys turned back and approached the building from the other side. They crossed the kitchen garden, skirted the woodshed and slipped into the basement through the window of the tuck-box room.

They avoided the main staircase and crept up the back stairs which brought them to the top landing at the rear of the building.

"Ssh! We're in open country now," Jennings whispered. "Can't you stop your shoes squeaking, Darbi?"

"Of course I can't—it's even more difficult than stopping your teeth from chattering," his friend replied. "And anyway, what about *your* shoes! They're going squelch-squelch every time you take a step and you're leaving wet footprints all along the passage. The sooner you get your feet dehydrated, the better."

They reached the dormitory without being seen and Darbishire's voice sounded confident again as he said: "Well, we've got here all right. It ought to be plain sailing from now on."

"Don't talk to me about sailing—plain or coloured. I've had enough for one day. You get my dry things out while I take this wet clutter off." Jennings walked into the dormitory and started to undress; his jacket dropped to the floor with the "plop" of a wet dishcloth.

"Bod and Ven need their brains seeing to," Darbishire remarked as he made for his friend's locker. "If they can't see your cupboard when it's bang in the middle of the room with your name on it, they must be bats."

"D'you mean crazy, or as blind as bats?"

"Both. I'll chuck your dry things . . ." For a moment there was silence, and then Darbishire's cry of amazement rang round the room. "Oh, gosh! Jennings! Oh, golly—they're not here!"

"What!" Jennings came rushing over and looked aghast at the empty locker. Not quite empty, however, for on the bottom shelf was a pair of pyjamas and six clean handkerchiefs; but his every-day suit, his shirt, his underwear—everything needed for a change of clothes was missing.

"So they must have taken them, after all," he said bitterly. "But where to? We know they haven't gone to the hut again, or we'd have met them coming back."

"No, we'd have met them *going*. They couldn't be coming back because they . . ." Darbishire broke off; someone was approaching the dormitory door.

Jennings grabbed his wet jacket and crouched between the beds. If this was the master on duty making a surprise inspection of the dormitories, there was just a chance that he would not look . . .

The door opened and Temple walked in.

"Oh, there you are!" he said as Jennings raised his head. "I wondered whether you'd come back."

"I should jolly well think I *have* come back," exclaimed Jennings angrily. "You and Venables are ozard cads, leaving me to suffer like that. If I'd stayed out there any longer, I should have fossilised into an icicle."

"Yes, well, sorry about that, but something went wrong." Briefly, Temple explained the plan that had been forced upon them; explained, that is, until he reached the point in the story where he had hurried downstairs to await Venables' arrival by the bootlockers.

What had happened after that, Temple did not know; he had waited and waited and Venables had not come. Then he had searched for him—still without result. In Temple's mind, the extraordinary disappearance of his friend ranked high amongst the great unsolved mysteries of the age, and until this problem was solved, Jennings' dry clothes would have to be regarded as lost in transit.

It was a dismal story, but worse was to come. "And Old Wilkie wants to know why you two and Venables haven't reported that you're back from your walk," Temple went on. "Everyone else got themselves ticked off hours ago, and Wilkie's charging round like a bull going *doyng* in a china shop, looking for you."

Darbishire looked at the sodden figure of his friend with sympathy and said: "We'll have to go and report, Jen. When Mr. Wilkins gets into one of his famous bates, he's worse than fifty-three Spanish men-o'-war with their battle thunder and flame."

"But I can't go like this! Do you think I could get into one of your suits?"

"Gosh, no!" replied Temple. "I'm fatter than you, and Darbi's too small. You'd look like a pumpkin in a peanut shell. Wilkie would spot it at once."

Their luck was no better when they searched Venables'

82

and Atkinson's lockers, for the owners' week-day suits had been taken to the sewing-room for minor repairs.

The situation seemed hopeless, and as the three boys stood debating what was to be done, a heavy tread was heard on the landing below and the loud tones of the master on duty floated up the stairs and through the open door. "Who's that up there in Dormitory 4?" called Mr. Wilkins.

Jennings flashed a glance at Darbishire. "Try and head him off," the glance said, and Darbishire walked out on to the landing.

"It's me, sir! Darbishire, sir! I've just come back from the walk. Will you tick me off, please, sir?" he said.

Mr. Wilkins ticked him off in no uncertain terms. "You're nearly ten minutes late reporting," he said, amongst other things. "And where are Venables and Jennings?"

"Jennings is in here, sir. Will you tick him off too, please, sir?"

Mr. Wilkins bristled: the rules of the school concerning Sunday walks were quite plain—each boy had to report personally to the master on duty. "If Jennings is there," he barked, "you can tell him that I'll give him just one minute to report to me in my room. And if he's not there then, I'll—I'll—well, he'd better look out! "

Mr. Wilkins strode off along the landing and a moment later the door of his room banged noisily behind him.

CHAPTER EIGHT

The Small Back Room

As THE last seconds of the minute of grace ticked away, there was a knock on Mr. Wilkins' door. "Come in!" he called.

"It's only me, sir; Jennings, sir," came a reluctant voice from without. "I won't trouble you by coming in, sir. I just wanted to report that I've come back."

Mr. Wilkins frowned at the door panels. It was something new in his experience that Jennings did not wish to put the master on duty to any trouble. "Open the door and come in properly," he boomed. "Don't stand outside gibbering at me through the keyhole. I've been searching the building for the last . . ."

The door opened and a familiar figure walked in, with a self-conscious look on his face. Although it was just after four o'clock in the afternoon, the new arrival was wearing a dressing-gown and pyjamas.

"I . . . I . . . Corwumph! What on earth's the meaning of this?" demanded Mr. Wilkins.

"You told me to report to you, sir. You see, I've just got back, sir."

"You didn't go for a walk in your pyjamas, did you?"

"No, sir; I had to change. That's why I'm a little late in reporting. You see, sir, my best suit got a few spots of damp on it, sir."

"Spots of damp! Why should it? It's not raining."

Jennings looked out of the window; unfortunately the sun was shining again now. Would Mr. Wilkins *never* stop asking questions to which there were no answers—unless

84

the whole colony of squatters was to suffer for the misfortunes of a single member?

"No, it's not actually raining, sir," Jennings admitted, "but the weather looked a bit unsettled, so I thought it might be better to change first and be on the safe side."

It was not a very convincing answer and Mr. Wilkins' eyebrows shot up and he turned three shades pinker. "But you—you *silly* little boy," he expostulated, "you—you uncouth youth. Why put your pyjamas on before the rain starts? I—I mean, why put them on at all? It's perfectly dry outside, and even if it wasn't, you could have changed into your week-day suit."

"I couldn't do that, sir; Venables is wearing it."

"What! Whatever for? Hasn't he got one of his own?"

"Yes, sir, and he's wearing that too—his own Sunday suit, that is, and a few of my other clothes as well."

"I—I—Corwumph! Don't talk such ridiculous nonsense! "

Mr. Wilkins rose from his chair and paced the room with his hand to his head. Why couldn't small boys say what they meant without dragging in so many things which had nothing to do with the topic under discussion? This didn't make sense, whichever way he looked at it; he was still searching his mind for some reason why Jennings should put his pyjamas on because the weather was unsettled, and now the issue was being clouded by Venables taking his afternoon stroll, clad in layer upon layer of grey flannel suiting!

Mr. Wilkins decided that he could solve this problem only if he kept very calm and took everything in its right order.

"Now, look here, Jennings! " he said reasonably. "How on earth can anyone be wearing your week-day suit on a Sunday, as well as his own Sunday suit on a week day? I mean, er—well, you heard what I said. What I want to know is, why is Venables wearing your suit?"

"Because we're both about the same size, sir."

Mr. Wilkins shut his eyes and gritted his teeth. He was not a patient man by nature, but no one could say that he was not doing his best in difficult circumstances. "Where is Venables?" he asked weakly.

"He's disappeared, sir."

"Oh, he has, has he! Well, listen to me. I don't know what all this dressing-up in dressing-gown nonsense is all about, but I'm not going to have it. You'll go and find this vanishing Venables at once; get your Sunday suit from him and report back to me wearing it."

"But Venables hasn't got my Sunday suit, sir."

All Mr. Wilkins' resolutions about patience and forbearance vanished in an explosion of exasperation. "But you—you *silly* little boy—you just told me that he *had*!"

"No, sir. He's got my week-day one, sir. P'r'aps I'd better explain from the beginning."

He had not proceeded far with his explanation before there was a knock at the door, and Matron and Mr. Carter joined them. Matron was carrying the missing clothes over her arm and in the interval before the door closed, Jennings caught a glimpse of Venables signalling sorrowfully to him from the corridor. His smile of apology was wan and he twisted his fingers with embarrassment and remorse.

Matron's concern was all for Jennings' welfare, but Mr. Carter had had a fruitless journey to the hut and he was not looking very pleased. He did, however, have the advantage over his colleague of knowing what the trouble was all about.

"Thank goodness you've come!" Mr. Wilkins greeted them. "I can't make head or tail of this trumpery moonshine about Tennyson's *Revenge* and a yachting club. All I know is that this boy reported to me wearing his dressing-gown. What do you make of that?"

"I think it's very intelligent of him," Matron answered unexpectedly. "It's not every boy who would have thought of getting ready for a bath without being told."

"Bath? At this time of day!" queried Mr. Wilkins. "Whatever for? Hasn't he had one lately?"

"I've had one, sir," Jennings admitted. "Sort of accidentally in the pond, sir."

Sternly, Mr. Carter said: "We'll talk about the cold bath

86

after you've had your hot one, Jennings. Matron's orders are that you have it at once and make sure the water's hot."

"Yes, sir." Jennings took his clothes and departed thankfully for the bathroom. When the door had closed behind him, Mr. Wilkins sighed deeply and said: "Well, I don't understand what it's all about, but it strikes me that's a rather unnecessary sort of order, Matron."

Matron looked puzzled. "Why?" she inquired.

"Well, you don't have to tell a boy like Jennings to get into hot water, I mean, dash it, he's in hot water all the time!"

It cannot truthfully be said that the four members of the yachting club enjoyed that Sunday evening. After chapel, Mr. Carter sent for them and although he could sympathise with good intentions, he could not shut his eyes to breaches of school rules. Thus it was not Jennings' accidental plunge which worried Mr. Carter; it was the fact that they had not observed the rule about going for a walk.

For the rest of the term, he decreed, they would not be allowed out by themselves, and on Sundays they would have to accompany Binns and his cronies on the Form 1 walk—a shrill-voiced crocodile which set forth in charge of a master.

This was punishment indeed, for the indignity of being shepherded about with eight-year-olds would be heightened by the mocking comments of their own colleagues in Form 3. Even the shallowest bonehead would be able to think of some apt and unkind remarks to add to their discomfort.

In addition to this, Jennings was to pay with his own pocket-money for the cleaning of his best suit. Mr. Carter made an entry in his cash book and the account of J. C. T. Jennings was reduced by fifty pence.

"With regard to the huts," Mr. Carter finished up, "I shall leave the decision to the Headmaster, and until you hear what he intends to do about them, you may carry on as usual."

The Headmaster made no reference to the huts when he gave out the orders for the day at breakfast the follow-

87

ing morning. Jennings and Darbishire listened with their fingers crossed and breathed a sigh of relief when the period of danger was over. Was it possible, they wondered, that the Headmaster considered that they had been punished enough already and was not going to take further action?

That evening, after preparation, they went across to the little hut as usual. Jennings took with him two pieces of broken mirror which he had found in the waste-paper basket and which, if skilfully handled, would convert the ventilating-shaft into a periscope. They worked on it for some time without success and finally they had to dismantle the shaft altogether.

'It's this bent bit in the middle that's the trouble," Darbishire decided. "When you bunged your famous two-way ear-trumpet into it you must have bashed it up a bit, and any fool knows you can't see round corners."

"Well, what are we wasting our time making a periscope for, then?" demanded Jennings.

"So's we can see round corners."

"You just said we couldn't!"

"Ah, but what I meant was—well, never mind. I vote we take the shaft outside and straighten it before we start the heavy construction work. There's a good chance the roof won't fall down, if we bung a stick or something in its place for the time being."

The periscope very nearly worked when it was finished. One piece of mirror was wedged in the top of the shaft at an acute angle, and the second piece was placed in the ear-trumpet, half-way down. Those with keen eyesight were almost sure that they could see objects moving at a distance.

Darbishire's eyesight was not keen, but his imagination was good. "I can see someone coming across the suspension bridge," he exclaimed as he peered into the lower mirror. "It looks like Binns to me."

It was not Binns. It was M. W. B. Pemberton-Oakes, Esq., M.A. (Oxon.), Headmaster, and he was coming to make a personal inspection of the activities by the pond.

His first thought, when he had heard of the yachting fiasco, had been to place the whole area out of bounds, but he had postponed his decision when Mr. Carter had spoken strongly on the hut-dwellers' behalf. Indeed, the boys would have been surprised if they could have heard how persuasively Mr. Carter had argued as he sat in the Headmaster's study that morning. He had pointed out that hut building was an admirable outlet for the surplus energy which bubbles up in boys like water in a pressure-cooker; he had touched upon the advantages of healthy exercise and upon the joy of home-made possessions—a joy which was out of all proportion to the value of the objects possessed. Mr. Carter had not stressed the educational value of the enterprise, for he doubted whether there was much to be learned from squatting in wattle igloos and eating walnut cake and sardines; but for a harmless relaxation there seemed no better way of spending the odd hour before bedtime.

"Harmless?" queried the Headmaster. "You seem to forget, Carter, that we're discussing this subject mainly because one boy has soiled a perfectly good suit."

"I don't think that will happen again," Mr. Carter replied. "Admittedly, they were extremely foolish, but I feel it would be a pity to come down too heavily on them merely because of one lapse."

"H'm!" The Headmaster paced his study thoughtfully. "I shall go and see for myself exactly what *is* happening over there. Until I have done so, I shall keep an open mind on the subject. Whether I allow the activities to continue after my visit will depend upon whether I form a favourable impression of what I see."

Unfortunately, the first thing the Headmaster saw on his way to the huts was the suspension bridge, and the first impression he formed was that it would bear his weight.

He had reached the middle of the bridge when it started to sink slowly into the quagmire beneath. For a moment he hesitated; then with a leap such as he had not attempted

89

since his undergraduate days, he cleared the remaining distance in a bound. The bridge, relieved of his weight, rose slowly from the mud to its normal height.

It was then that Darbishire made the discovery with the periscope and spun round to see who the visitor really was. "Golly, it's the Archbeako!" he exclaimed. "I wonder what he's come beetling over here for!"

"I can guess," Jennings answered. "And the less yachting equipment he sees lying about, the better. Where's the *Revenge*?"

"It's in the small back room."

"Well, cover it up with the door-mat then, and try and look as though you're engaged on important research work on the life cycle of tadpoles."

"But I don't know anything about tadpoles. I didn't even know they had cycles," Darbishire pointed out.

"They don't have cycles—they go in them."

"Don't you mean they go *on* them?"

"Oh, don't be such a bogus bazooka, Darbi! Buck up, he's coming!" Jennings thrust the *Welcome* mat into his friend's hands and pushed him into the small back room. He returned the ventilating-shaft to its usual work of propping up the roof, and then he glanced quickly round the hut. Everything was in order; provided that the conversation was kept away from sailing and model yachts, there was nothing to prevent the Headmaster's visit from being enjoyed by all parties.

The word had passed from hut to hut: "Archbeako on the prowl!" and everywhere a frantic tidying-up was in progress; Brown major cleaned his muddy shoes on a tuft of grass; Binns minor, who was up a tree piloting a jet-fighter, parachuted to the ground without even waiting for the signal from his control tower to land on the runway; Rumbelow grabbed a school text book which he had been using to block up a hole in the roof of his hut, and sought a safe hiding-place for it beneath his jacket. No effort was spared to give the unexpected visitor a favourable impression.

Mr. Pemberton-Oakes walked slowly across from the

bridge, his keen eye taking in every detail of the scene. His first real surprise was when a bodiless head suddenly appeared in the long grass at his feet. It smiled politely and said: "Good evening, sir," before it disappeared into the ground like a fox going to earth.

The Headmaster's surprise was natural, for it was the first time he had seen Bromwich looking out from the front door of his semi-basement elephant trap. Bromwich, now happily restored to health, returned to his living-room and told Elmer to behave himself because a distinguished visitor was in the offing.

The distinguished visitor moved on and glanced into each hut as he passed. The squatters gave him smiles of welcome; they had ceased all active and noisy pursuits and were trying to look as though their greatest pleasure was to stand in respectful silence and listen to the croaking of the frogs in the pond. When Mr. Pemberton-Oakes reached Jennings' little hut, he stopped.

"Good evening, sir!" said Jennings and Darbishire in restrained tones.

"Good evening! So these are the huts of which Mr. Carter speaks so highly! H'm! I cannot think why you should choose the muddiest corner of the school grounds for the erection of these—ah—sorry-looking shanties of twig and bulrush. I am further at a loss to understand, Jennings, why you should be standing in a puddle with only one shoe on."

"I'm sorry, sir! I didn't notice the puddle; and I've been using my other shoe to hammer our periscope into shape, sir."

"Really! And where is your tie, Darbishire?"

"It's—er, I know it's about somewhere, sir." It was difficult to explain, without going into technical details, that his tie was an important part of a patent window-opening device; and somehow Darbishire did not think that the Headmaster was in the mood for technical details.

"I have come over here to satisfy myself that these huts are a suitable feature of our out-of-school activites," the Headmaster went on. "So far, I have seen little evidence to support such a belief. This, I gather, is your hut, Jennings?"

"Mine and Darbishire's, sir."

"Mine and Darbishire's!" repeated the Headmaster in a shocked voice. "I should have thought, Jennings, that the elementary knowledge of English grammar which even you possess, would have prompted you to say, 'Darbishire's and mine'."

"Yes, sir."

No one could say that Mr. Pemberton-Oakes was not thorough. At the expense of a ruffled dignity and damp patches on both knees, he crawled inside the little hut to make a closer inspection. Jennings and Darbishire stood outside anxiously, listening to the muffled sounds which came from within.

"This is ozard egg, isn't it?" whispered Jennings. "He seems in a bit of a bate, too. I hope he doesn't stop us coming here."

"We needn't despair yet," Darbishire muttered from the corner of his mouth. "My father says that you should never meet trouble half-way, and there's just a chance that . . . Gosh, what*ever* is he doing?"

They strained their ears, trying to follow their visitor's progress from the sounds that filtered out through the door, but as they could see nothing, they could only guess at what was really happening inside.

In point of fact, very little was happening. The Headmaster found nothing to which he could take exception and he had decided that perhaps Mr. Carter was right and there was, after all, no reason why these innocent pleasures should not be followed in moderation. A closer supervision by the master on duty would be advisable, but that could easily be arranged.

If the Headmaster had left the hut then and there while his mind was still full of favourable impressions, all might have been well; but it was not to be. He was on the point of leaving when he noticed the hole leading to the small back room. Now, what could that be? Perhaps he had better investigate; a quick glance would be sufficient, for he was ruining the knees of his trousers, and the sooner he could stand upright, the better.

Mr. Pemberton-Oakes was half-way through the entrance to the small back room when he realised that he was stuck. After all, the hole was designed for small inventors only, and for a fully-grown adult to try to force his way through was asking for trouble. The Headmaster tried to move forwards and a shower of reeds and brambles fell upon him from the roof; he tried to move backwards, and the movement loosened the ventilating-shaft which Jennings had not had time to replace securely.

There was no doubt about it—Mr. Pemberton-Oakes was securely wedged on all sides. Distinctly annoyed, he tried to struggle to his feet and force his way out by sheer strength. As he rose, the walls rose with him, the roof caved in and the ventilating-shaft toppled forward, pinning him to the ground in a welter of branches, bulrushes and home-made furniture.

A sack-like object dropped from above and landed a short distance in front of him. The Headmaster could not move, but he could see: and what he saw on the sack-like object did nothing to improve his feelings: *Welcome to Ye Oldë Worldë Huttë*, it said.

Jennings and Darbishire watched with mounting horror. Earthquakes and landslides seemed to be happening before their eyes; the little hut was heaving like a thing possessed, and they were powerless to do anything about it.

"Oh, golly!" breathed Jennings in dismay. "He's smashing the place up like a bulldozer. I knew the roof wasn't safe—I hadn't got time to bung the shaft back properly."

"He seems to have got stuck in the back-room boys' department," said Darbishire, and timorously he called: "Er, are you quite all right, sir?"

Their visitor was not quite all right, and Jennings decided to take action. "Come on, Darbi, we'll have to rescue him before he does any more demolition work!" But it was difficult to know where to start.

The rescue party was soon joined by a score of volunteers from neighbouring huts. They arrived demanding to know what was going on, and their crisp comments on the situation had to be quickly and sternly silenced; for though the Headmaster was not in sight, he was only too plainly within earshot.

"We'll have to take the roof off," Jennings announced, and in a lower tone, he added: "Buck up, you chaps, for goodness' sake. He's done as much damage as three atom bombs already, and if he puts his foot through the ventilating-shaft, we'll never be able to use it as a periscope."

The willing hands went to work and soon the snapping of branches told that the work of rescue was getting under way.

"This is ozard," groaned Darbishire, as he helped to lift the roof. "He's bound to be in the most frantic bate when he gets out. My father says that one woe doth tread upon another's heels, so fast they . . ."

"Well, stop treading on *my* heels and help me get this branch out of the light," suggested Atkinson. He was red in the face with the exertion and he was enjoying every minute of it. But after all, he could afford to—it was not *his* hut.

A minute later, Mr. Pemberton-Oakes arose from the ruins and shook stray twigs and brambles from his clothing. His feet were damp, for the emergency drinking supply had been overturned when the walls collapsed; his tie was awry and his hair was untidy, but his face showed no sign of emotion. The rescuers noted this and fell silent, for everyone knew that the more deeply the Headmaster felt upon a subject, the less he showed his feelings in his expression.

Finally, he spoke. "This area of the grounds will be placed out of bounds for the entire school forthwith," he began. "From what I have seen, I consider that the building of huts is not a suitable occupation for boys of your age. Your clothes are untidy, your boots are dirty and if you are permitted to continue in this way, unchecked, it will undermine the pride which you should be taking in your personal appearance. You will all return to school and set to work with clothes-brush and boot polish to make yourselves presentable." He paused, and a far-away look appeared for a second in his eyes before he went on: "Of what has happened since I arrived, I shall, for the moment, say nothing."

With heavy hearts the squatters turned and made for the school buildings. So that was the end of the huts! And all thanks to Jennings!

"It *would* be Jennings who had to go and bish it up for everybody," grumbled Thompson minor.

"Huh! Just like Jennings to make a hut that falls down *doyng* as soon as the Archbeako beetles inside!" moaned Rumbelow.

"Gosh, Jennings, you *are* a ruin!" The evening air was heavy with reproaches—low-toned criticism which was not supposed to reach the Headmaster's ear.

Mr. Pemberton-Oakes waited by the huts until all the boys had disappeared in the direction of the school buildings. Somehow or other he had got to get back across the pontoon-suspension bridge, and he had no intention of doing *that* in front of an audience!

CHAPTER NINE

England Wins the Ashes

IN THE dormitories that evening, Jennings found himself the centre of a swirling cyclone of resentment. Oddly enough, his critics did not blame him for short-circuiting the Sunday walk or for spoiling his best suit in the pond—they could sympathise with things like that. But what really infuriated them was the fact that his hut should have collapsed on the Headmaster; this, they maintained, was the cause of the ban, and the blame for it must be laid at Jennings' door.

"I'm just about fed up with you, Jennings," said Temple, as he undressed. "All that guff we had to put up with about your famous two-roomed hut standing in its own grounds—and then it goes and sits down in them while the Archbeako's paying us a friendly visit."

Venables added an unfriendly glance and said: "You're an ozard swizzler, Jennings. To think Bod and I actually sat inside that tottering ruin of yours, eating walnut cake and sardines! We might have been buried alive any moment." He shivered at the thought of his narrow escape.

"I couldn't help it," Jennings protested. "That small back room wasn't built for grown-ups of riper years. And, anyway, if he'd kept still and not shoved like the back row of a rugger scrum, we'd have had him out without any hoo-hah."

Atkinson looked up from the washbasin. "Don't make feeble excuses! You've made a frantic bish of the whole issue. I bet no one else's hut would have pancaked if the old man had gone inside."

96

Loyally Darbishire came to his friend's assistance. "Don't you be so sure," he said. "If he'd walked two inches more to the left when he was coming across, he'd have gone *slap-bang-doyng* through Bromo's roof and perhaps even landed up in the goldfish tank."

As junior partner in the little hut Darbishire came in for a certain amount of reproach, and it seemed unfair to him that Venables and Temple, who had been as keen as anyone on the yachting expedition, should now put all the blame on the owners of the unfortunate shanty. Surely they could see that no building of reeds and branches could withstand the bulldozing tactics of a fully-grown headmaster.

Mr. Carter was on dormitory duty that evening, and he was quick to sense that the usual, friendly atmosphere of bedtime was missing. There was little he could do about it, though he was very short with anyone who had more to say about the subject than was necessary.

When the boys were in bed, Mr. Carter called for silence and then made his way to the Headmaster's study. He often went there in the evenings to discuss the events of the day and the plans for the morrow.

"Come in and sit down, Carter," the Headmaster greeted him. "I'm just finishing off a notice."

The school secretary was away that day and Mr. Pemberton-Oakes was trying his hand at typing. It was the first time he had done so, and he was making less progress than he had hoped.

Mr. Carter sat in an arm-chair and glanced at the evening paper while the Headmaster turned again to his typewriter. It was slow work, but he persevered, and at five-second intervals the silence was broken as one more letter was tapped, on to the sheet of paper in the machine.

"Tut-tut-tut! I'd no idea that typing was so difficult," observed Mr. Pemberton-Oakes. "My secretary dashes these things off without even looking at the keyboard. Now where on earth is the comma—I'm sure I saw one somewhere! . . . Ah, yes, here it is . . . Oh dear, how unfortunate —it's turned itself into a question mark!"

"Can I help?" volunteered Mr. Carter, laying down the newspaper.

"Oh, no, thank you! I'm just typing a memorandum to pin up on the notice board." And three minutes later he added: "On second thoughts it would be considerably quicker to write it out by hand. Somehow, I don't think that this quite conveys my meaning." He rolled the paper from the machine and passed it to his assistant.

"NOT ICE," it read. "In fiyutre no buys will be preMnitted to bluild nuts ub the neiHghbourhoof uf the pond? & the a£5rea will be plAvced ou98t of hounds$\frac{1}{2}$%."

"You're quite right," Mr. Carter agreed. "I think I know what you mean, but it's a little obscure in parts."

The Headmaster tore it up, and as he dropped the pieces in the wastepaper-basket he said: "It must be very useful to know how to type. However, perhaps you would pass it round amongst the staff, that in future no boys will be permitted to build huts. I'm placing the whole area of the pond out of bounds from now on, because I'm unable to agree that this particular form of recreation serves any useful purpose." He pursed his lips and shook his head slowly. "Any visitor going round the school, Carter, and seeing the boys in the untidy and dishevelled state they were in this evening would be certain to form the most unfavourable impressions."

Mr. Carter agreed about the visitors, but he pointed out that he always insisted upon the boys making themselves presentable as soon as they arrived back in the school buildings.

The Headmaster was not satisfied. "I've no doubt you do, Carter, but it still isn't good enough. It is essential that the boys should pursue their outdoor hobbies in a neat and orderly manner. This morning, for instance, I had a letter from General Merridew; he's bringing his daughter-in-law and his grandson down to see the school next Friday. Frankly, I shudder to think of the General's remarks if he found that the boys were not looking as smart as they did when he was a boy at school, here."

"Is the grandson coming to us as a boarder?" inquired Mr. Carter.

"I hope so. He will be entered as a new boy for next term, provided that his mother is satisfied with what we have to show her. The choice of school rests with her because the boy's father is stationed abroad in the Navy. I should like young Roger to come here; his father was an Old Linburian and so, of course, was his grandfather."

Mr. Carter had met the grandfather on several occasions. Lieut.-General Sir Melville Merridew, Bart., D.S.O., M.C., was one of the most distinguished of all the Old Boys who had spent their early years at Linbury, and as the donor of the *Merridew Inter-House Sports Cup*, he was a notable figure at every Speech Day gathering.

The Headmaster picked up the General's letter from his desk and quoted: "My grandson, Roger, is nearly eight years old and I am keen to carry on the family tradition and send him to Linbury. In my view it is high time that the lad went to his preparatory school and had a few of the rough corners knocked off him. However, his mother must make the decision, not me, so I shall bring her and the boy along next Friday if this is convenient."

Mr. Pemberton-Oakes laid down the letter and turned to his assistant. "I am determined that General Merridew shall not be disappointed," he said. "He is a man of high standards and he expects the best, so we must ensure that everything he sees affords him and Mrs. Merridew the utmost satisfaction. I gather, from what the General told me last term, that Roger is—ah—how shall I put it? Well, he is a high-spirited child and his mother has always allowed him to do very much as he pleases."

Mr. Carter nodded; he had met that sort of boy before and he knew that after a very short space of time, the newcomer would find his feet and appear little different from his fellows. It was surprising how easily the spoiled, the highly-strung and the "difficult" boy forgot his temperamental moods when once he found himself part of the little world of boarding-school life.

"I shall show the General's party all over the school and

all over the grounds so that they may see things for themselves," the Headmaster went on. "Now, perhaps, you understand why it would be inadvisable to allow the boys to continue their games by the pond. Can you imagine a man like General Merridew entering his grandson for a preparatory school where the boys are plastered in mud from ankle to eyebrow?"

"Perhaps not," Mr. Carter agreed. "But if they see the school running normally, they'll be able to judge our methods for themselves and they'll be bound to agree that the boys are very happy here."

The Headmaster strolled over to the window, where he stood enjoying the cool night air. At length, he said: "I rather think, Carter, that something more than that is called for. Knowing General Merridew as well as I do, I feel that next Friday will be an occasion that demands something more than the normal effort. The building must be tidied from top to bottom and the grounds swept from end to end; the boys will wear their best suits and I shall ask Matron to see that no boy needs his hair cut or wears shoes which are in need of repair."

"M'yes, but . . ." Mr. Carter began doubtfully, but the Headmaster was in full spate and was in no mood to be interrupted. "I will see the house-keeper in the morning," he went on. "Luncheon next Friday must be prepared with particular care. Tablecloths, of course, and clean napkins for the boys; now what do you think, Carter, about a vase of flowers on all the dining-hall tables?"

"I think it would be a mistake. I think your visitors would be able to form a better opinion of the school if they see us as we usually are."

"In this case, I think not," replied Mr. Pemberton-Oakes. "The General has a right to expect the best from his old school and we should be failing in our duty if we did not provide it. Yes, Carter, I'm determined to see that no effort is spared in making a favourable impression on General Merridew and his party."

Jennings and Darbishire were the last to reach the cricket

field after preparation on Wednesday evening. As they were crossing the quad, Jennings said: "I'll give you some coaching as we can't go to the hut, Darbi. Heaven knows you need it badly enough—you bowl like a flat-footed newt!"

Darbishire clutched his cricket bat and made no answer. There *was* no answer as far as his bowling was concerned, and he knew it.

All the cricket nets were occupied when they arrived and Jennings made for one at the far end where the other members of Dormitory 4 were disputing an l.b.w. decision. The argument revolved round the point of whether Atkinson could be "out" if the ball had struck him above the shoulder. Temple maintained that he could.

"But it can't be l.b.w., Bod—you got me on the nose," Atkinson protested.

"Well, you shouldn't stick your nose in front of the wicket," came the reasoned reply.

"It was your fault for bowling a sneak. I had to get down to it and then it jumped up and bashed me on the bonce."

"It's time you were out, anyway, Atki," Venables chimed in; as next man in, he was not in favour of giving the batsman the benefit of any doubt. "After all, you'd have been caught at cover point off the ball before if we'd had a fielder and the net hadn't stopped it."

"You're bats! I hit it to leg, and cover point's on the off."

"Ah, but if you'd been left-handed, cover point would have been fielding on the other side."

The argument seemed as though it might last for ever, so Jennings called out loudly: "I say, you chaps, can Darbi and I play in your net?"

The players ceased arguing and joined forces against the new enemy.

"No, you can't," said Temple curtly. His attitude plainly indicated that people who put other people to great inconvenience by building huts which folded up like opera hats at awkward moments could expect no favours. Venables and Atkinson nodded in agreement.

"But there's nowhere else we can play. All the other nets are full up," Jennings pointed out.

"That's your bad luck," retorted Atkinson. "Anyway, it's hopeless letting Darbishire play—he's such a rotten bat."

"You mean he's *got* a rotten bat, not he *is* one," Venables corrected.

"No, I don't. It's an expression like, say, for instance . . ."

"My bat isn't a rotten one," Darbishire defended himself. "My father made 17 not out with it, last year when he was playing for our village, so that'll show you!"

Temple, Venables and Atkinson hooted with laughter. "Gosh, Darbi, that's an ozard feeble sort of score. Couldn't he do better than that?" asked Venables.

"Oh, yes, he made 236 all in boundaries once."

"Phew! Not bad!" Atkinson was impressed. "Who was he playing against?"

"Well, that time he was playing on the beach and my mother was bowling with a tennis ball, but it proves my bat isn't so feeble as you make out."

"Well, anyway, you can't play here," said Temple. "We got here first and bagged this net just for us three."

Jennings and Darbishire did not argue, for it was plain that they were not wanted. The week had not been going well for them; Sunday had seen the sailing disaster, on Monday the huts were banned and the next morning a long-expected tuck parcel had arrived from Jennings' mother. Normally this would have been regarded as a red-letter day, but the food had been specially ear-marked for a feast in the little hut and it had arrived too late.

Sorrowfully they trudged away from the nets, towards the hedge which surrounded the Headmaster's garden. "What about this coaching, Darbi—shall we have a bash at it here?" Jennings asked.

"It's a bit near the Beako's garden," Darbishire demurred. "What if I walloped a ball over the hedge?"

Jennings laughed. "I can just see you doing that! Dash it all, Darbi, you couldn't even hit the side of a house with a bulldozer. I know," he went on. "Let's have a Test Match. You be Australia and I'll be England."

"That's not fair," Darbishire protested. "I'm *always* Australia. I'm never allowed to be England."

"Of course not. You're not good enough to play for England. Besides, the Australians are better really—they nearly always win the Ashes."

Darbishire frowned hard at his cricket bat while he sought for the flaw in this argument. Then he said: "Yes, but if I'm not good enough to play for England, why am I good enough to play for Australia, if they're better?"

"Because, if you're playing for Australia, England will be able to win the Ashes, so if you're patriotic you ought to be proud to help your country like that."

They had not brought any stumps with them, so they piled up their jackets to make a wicket, and Darbishire stripped for the match, still complaining that he had been chosen for the wrong side. Jenning's appeal to his patriotism had made things more difficult, for it seemed to suggest that he should play for one team while hoping that his opponents would win.

"I'll tell you what let's do, then," the England captain said graciously, but ungrammatically. "Australia can bat first and if they're out first ball, England will put them in again. That's fair enough, isn't it?"

He paced out the pitch while the Australian opening batsman took his stance at the wicket and made a few graceful practice strokes in the air. To fit himself for his part, he hummed a few bars of *Waltzing Matilda* and raised his imaginary cap to an imaginary crowd who were clapping till their imaginary palms ached.

At the other end of the pitch, Jennings was swinging his arm round and round to generate the current for his first ball, when Bromwich's brother sped across from the nets.

"Message from Mr. Carter," he announced. "He says you characters are playing too near the Archbeako's garden, and he's going to take off on a roof-level attack if you don't budge farther off."

"Mr. Carter said that?"

"Well, he used different words, but that's what he meant. He says the Head's threatened to stop us playing here after prep if we go too near his hedge. Can't stop—I'm in next and Mr. Carter's in our net, bowling supersonic leg-spinners." And the messenger hurried off.

Jennings glanced round the cricket field, but he could see no other suitable place where an important Test Match could be held, for seventy-nine boys divided up into nearly twenty separate groups took up all the available space. What should he do? Perhaps if he moved his pitch, say, two or three yards to the left, he would be complying with instructions. He knew, of course, that this was not quite what Mr. Carter had meant, but it was a move in the right direction and, anyway, the master seemed too busily engaged with his leg-spinners to notice how his orders were being carried out.

Jennings trotted down the pitch to where the Australian opening batsman was now entertaining the imaginary crowd by balancing his bat on his chin.

"We've got to hoof farther off, Darbi," Jennings said. "Shift the wicket a couple of yards farther away from the hedge."

"All right. By the way, I vote you don't bowl your fastest, because I haven't got any pads."

"But this is a Test Match!" Jennings sounded shocked. "What would people think if Australia asked England to bowl easy ones at Lords in case they got a crack on the shin? Come on, let's get started!" He ran back to the bowling end. "Pla-ay!" he called, and the fight for the Ashes began in earnest.

The first ball was straight and slow; Darbishire missed it completely and looked round to see it nestling in the grey flannel wicket behind him.

"How's that? Out! Middle stump, first ball!" Jennings danced with delight. "Australia all out for nought—hurray!"

"You said first ball didn't count," the Australian team objected as it fielded the ball and threw it back.

"All right, then—we'll put you in again. Pla-ay!"

The Australian side fared no better in the second innings, which again lasted for only one ball. England was scornful. "Really, Darbi, you are feeble! What's the point of coming all the way from the other side of the world just to run away from the first ball you get! You'll never get a knighthood for your contribution to sport if you don't do better than that!"

"It's all very well to talk," replied Darbishire, "but chaps at Lords who get knighted for their cricket don't have to play without pads, and my father says that . . ."

"All right, all right! Let's get on with the game! We'll see if your bowling's any better than your batting."

As a leg-spin bowler, Darbishire had modelled himself on Mr. Carter and he never tired of trotting along the corridors copying the master's bowling action as he went. Twelve short steps, a shuffle, a little jump and over came the arm with a flexible twist of wrist and fingers. Darbishire could imitate the movements perfectly but, somehow, whenever he tried it with a ball in his hand, something went wrong.

He paced out the twelve steps and turned to face the batsman. "Pla-ay!" he sang out. As usual, his run up to the bowling crease was faultless, the shuffle and the little jump were faithfully carried out, but as soon as the ball left his hand it developed a will of its own and sailed off towards square leg.

"Wide!" said Jennings disgustedly. "You are a prehistoric remains, Darbi; you only do sneaks or wides."

The bowler's pride was hurt. "All right then, I won't bowl any more. We'll say the match is over and you've won."

"But it can't be over—I haven't hit the ball yet."

"Yes, but I didn't score any runs and now I've bowled a wide, so that's a run to you and England have won the Ashes."

This seemed a little hard on England, who was stamping his feet with impatience to have a good crack at the bowling, and finally Australia agreed to carry on.

The reason why the Old Country scored no runs in the first over was because the ball never came near the batsman. Sometimes it rolled three-quarters of the way along the pitch, but by the time Jennings had rushed out to meet it, it was as lifeless as a bed-knob.

"This is ozard," he complained, after five minutes thwarted batting. "How do you expect me to make supersonic strokes off double wides and balls that never get here! Try and pitch them up a bit more!"

It was then that Darbishire bowled a good-length ball. He ran the twelve steps, remembered the shuffle and jump and swung his arm over, quite convinced that this ball would fare no better than its fellows. And no one was more surprised than the bowler when it pitched well down the wicket and in a straight line with the makeshift stumps.

"Oh, good ball!" cried Jennings, and stepped forward and smote it with all his strength. It rose from his bat high into the air and curved away towards the hedge.

"Oh, good shot, Jen—wizard stroke," yelled Darbishire generously. "It's a six! It's going right over the . . ." He stopped, for a crash of glass from behind the hedge told where the ball had landed.

For a few seconds they stared at each other in bemused silence. Then Jennings said: "I say, Darbi, did you—did you hear anything, just then?"

"I—er, I fancy I *did* hear a sort of tinkle, yes," Darbishire admitted in a strained, unnatural voice.

Jennings forced himself to make an unpleasant decision. "Come on!" he said. "We'll have to fox into the Head's garden and see what it is."

For a moment, Darbishire held back, his mind seeking faint hopes to cling to as a drowning man clutches at straws: perhaps the crash had nothing to do with Jennings' beautiful leg-drive; perhaps a cat had upset a nest of flower-pots at the very moment that the ball had disappeared over the hedge; perhaps . . . Darbishire sighed. No amount of wishful thinking could alter the real cause of that crash. The horrible sound still rang in his ears.

"There's no point in going to see what it is," he reminded his friend. "I know already; it's the Head's cucumber frame—the one we hid behind last Sunday."

"Yes, but we can't leave the ball there. You are a ruin, Darbi, sending down a straight one like that—I couldn't help swiping it."

"Well, I like that! A moment ago you were moaning because they *weren't* straight."

A quick look round the cricket field showed that no one else had heard the crash of glass. The little groups were still bowling at one another, and the thwack of the batsmen came distantly from the nets. It seemed strange to Jennings that no one should have noticed what, to him, had sounded like a whole colony of glass-house dwellers disregarding the proverb about throwing stones; but no one was so much as glancing in their direction, so the two boys crept towards the gap in the hedge which they had found the previous Sunday. Jennings crawled through while Darbishire stayed outside and kept watch.

It was quiet in the garden, for the sounds of the cricket field were muffled by the thick branches of yew; quiet, but dangerous, for the Headmaster's garden was out of bounds. There, ahead of him, Jennings could see the cucumber frame, and as he hurried along the path towards it he knew what he would find. And he was right!

Of the three panes of glass which protected the cucumbers only two were intact. The middle pane was smashed to fragments, and lying amongst the cucumbers at the bottom was his cricket ball.

When Jennings emerged on the lawful side of the hedge a few moments later, Darbishire said: "Buck up, Mr. Carter's just blown the 'all-in'!"

"Okay, I'm coming!" Jennings slipped the cricket ball

into his pocket. "The whistle's late tonight. It should have gone five minutes ago, by my watch."

Darbishire clicked his teeth with annoyance. "Doesn't that just prove how everything's against us?" he said bitterly. "If he'd blown it on time, this wouldn't have happened; we should have been indoors by now, instead of wondering what on earth we're going to do about that busted hunk of glass."

CHAPTER TEN

Absent-Minded Aunt

IT WAS not until break the next morning that Jennings and Darbishire were able to discuss the new disaster in detail. Then, as soon as they were released from Mr. Wilkins' geography class, they made for the tuck-box room to talk the matter over. Fate, they agreed, was not even *trying* to be fair, for the last few days had brought far more than any average spell of bad luck.

They sat on Jennings' tuck-box, eating the remains of his parcel while Darbishire recalled all the wise words of his father about troubles and sorrows which followed thick and fast upon one another's heels. Normally, they would have had no hesitation in reporting the broken pane to Mr. Carter and offering to pay for the damage out of their pocket-money. But things were not normal that week; the disasters of Sunday and Monday had reduced their reputation to its lowest ebb—and if this new misfortune were to come to light, anything might happen.

"It's not only busting the glass, you see, Darbi," Jennings pointed out, "but we went on playing after Mr. Carter had told us to beetle off. If that gets into the headlines they'll stop the whole school from having cricket practice after prep." He sighed. "And it was such a super leg-drive, too! "

"And it was the first decent ball I've bowled this term," added Darbishire. "What an ozard swizz! Never mind, you got the Ashes—or the splinters, rather." He polished an apple on his sleeve and fell silent, for his friend was deep in thought.

For some moments Jennings sat turning over in his mind what was best to be done. The Headmaster had little time for gardening during the term, and as the frame was in a far corner there was a chance that the damage would not be discovered for some days. But it was bound to be noticed sooner or later, and then the trouble would start. Who broke this? Why were you playing so near the garden? Why didn't you move away when you were ordered to do so? And then the verdict—No boy is to practise cricket after evening preparation.

Jennings could imagine it all and hear the hostile comments of his colleagues. And, after all, he would deserve them, for twice in one week is rather too often for a third-former to bring a loss of privileges upon the whole school. Surely there must be some way out of the difficulty! If only the Headmaster could find an undamaged pane the next time he strolled round inspecting his vegetables. An idea took shape in Jennings' mind and he broke the silence by saying: "Do you happen to know of any decent glass shops in these parts, Darbi?"

Darbishire looked puzzled. "Do you mean ones that sell glass or ones with masses of windows?" he inquired.

"I was just wondering whether we could buy a hunk without saying a lot about it."

"Gosh, yes! " cried Darbishire; his eyes shone with enthusiasm. "What about the Linbury Stores in the village? They sell everything—saucepans, postcards, paraffin, sticking-plaster . . ."

"We don't want any saucepans, and sticking-plaster wouldn't be any good, anyway—that pane's in about five million small fragments."

"No, I didn't mean let's mend it. I meant a shop like that is sure to sell ordinary stuff like glass, isn't it?"

"Bound to," Jennings agreed. "Darbi, I think we're saved! "

They shook hands heartily and celebrated their salvation with a pineapple chunk apiece, from Jennings' parcel.

"All we've got to do," Jennings declared, "is to get some dosh out of the school bank, ask permish to beetle down to the village and buy a nice new slab of the right size."

"Bags you do it, then," replied Darbishire, wiping his sticky fingers on his tie. "I wouldn't know what to ask for."

"Don't be so bats—you just ask for glass."

"Yes, but they might have different sorts—frosted, or powdered—or stained-glass, even; and besides, do they sell it by weight or so many panes for five pence?"

"Leave it to me!" said Jennings. "I'll nip back into the garden after lunch and measure it up; and after school this afternoon we'll go and ask Mr. Carter for some pocket-money."

Mr. Carter was marking exercise books when the knock sounded on his study door. He had already guessed who his visitors were from the whispered conversation which had been going on outside his room for the previous five minutes. The words were inaudible, but the high-pitched tone of the whisperers was unmistakable. "A secret and important plan is going to be carried out," the urgent undertones informed him.

Very few things happened at Linbury which escaped Mr. Carter's attention, and when his visitors entered he had no difficulty in seeing through the masks of innocence which veiled their faces. Either something had happened, or something was going to happen, Mr. Carter decided, and filed the observation away in his mind until it should be needed.

"Oh, yes, I want to see you, Jennings," the master said. "I sent a message to you yesterday evening to move your pitch away from the Head's garden. Did you do so?"

"We moved a little bit, sir," Jennings replied, "but there wasn't room to go far. We were having a private Test Match, you see, sir."

"I was Australia, sir," Darbishire added, "and England won by an innings and ten wickets. Australia made nought in both innings and England got one wide, sir."

"Really! Quite a phenomenal score," smiled Mr Carter.

"Of course, they do better at Lords, sir, but that's probably because they don't have to bat without pads." Darbishire suddenly wondered why he was telling his housemaster all these details; could it be that he was prattling about nothing in particular merely to postpone the serious business for which they had come? He forced himself back to the matter in hand and gave his friend an encouraging nudge. "Go on, Jennings!" he muttered.

"Well, sir," Jennings began, "what we really came to see you about was to ask for some of our pocket-money, sir."

Mr. Carter looked interested. "I opened the bank after lunch yesterday," he replied. "Why didn't you ask me then?"

"I didn't need it, then sir. You see—well, actually, sir, it's a bit urgent, if you see what I mean, sir. I think I need about forty pence."

Mr. Carter did not ask why. Instead he opened the cash book in which he kept records of the boys' bank balances. "Sorry! You've only got four pence left," he said.

"Only four pence, sir! But I had fifty-four pence the other day!"

"Quite right! But I deducted fifty to pay for your suit to go to the cleaners. Perhaps you'd forgotten."

Jennings had, and a wave of gloom splashed over him. Where on earth was the money to come from? His friend could not help either, for when Mr. Carter turned to the account, the balance in favour of C. E. J. Darbishire was exactly one pence.

"Oh, well, it can't be helped then, sir; sorry to trouble you, sir," said Jennings; but as he made for the door, Mr. Carter called him back and said: "If this matter is really urgent, Jennings, and you'd care to tell me about it, perhaps I could help."

Jennings wanted to tell him; desperately he wanted to shed the load of this new trouble which was making life so difficult.

"Well, sir," he said, and then stopped. It would be most unfair on the rest of the school if evening cricket was to be stopped; was it right that seventy-nine boys should suffer for the misfortunes of two of their number? "No thank you, sir," he finished up. "It's quite all right, really."

Mr. Carter sat and thought for some while after the boys had gone. Why were ten-year-olds so obstinate? Why wouldn't they say outright what the matter was, instead of putting themselves and everyone else to unnecessary trouble? One thing, however, seemed certain; this plan of theirs, whatever it was, had depended on their being able to withdraw some money from the bank. That had failed, so now, perhaps, their scheme would be abandoned.

So thought Mr. Carter. But, for once, he thought wrong!

Downstairs in the tuck-box room, Jennings and Darbishire sat and stared at each other in moody silence. At last, Darbishire said: "We've just *got* to do something! We can't buy any glass if we haven't got any dosh, so I vote we go back to Mr. Carter and tell him what's happened."

"That won't help," answered Jennings glumly. "We still can't pay for the damage and there'll be a hoo-hah for everyone on top of that."

"There'll be a hoo-hah, anyhow!" Darbishire's tone was gloomily confident. "As soon as the Archbeako ankles round his garden, he's going to say, 'Now, who's been bashing a ball over my hedge?' And then . . ."

Jennings jumped to his feet and suddenly the wide-awake look was back in his eyes. "I know!" he cried triumphantly. "My Aunt Angela!"

Darbishire looked doubtful. "Why, does she play cricket?"

"No, she plays croquet—at least she used to, about twenty years ago. Listen, Darbi, I think I've . . ."

"Don't be such a bogus bazooka!" his friend interrupted. "Why should the Head think the glass was smashed twenty years ago by your aunt playing croquet?"

"I didn't say that. I meant there's a decent chance that the letter will come tomorrow."

"What letter?"

"Aunt Angela's. You remember my Aunt Angela, don't you?"

"The old geezer who doesn't like cats?"

113

"Yes, that's right. Gosh, why didn't I think about her before?"

"Think *what* about her?"

Jennings explained. Every month, Aunt Angela wrote her nephew a letter, and once a term she enclosed a postal order for fifty pence. She was rather forgetful and had to be reminded, at times, and on the last occasion that Jennings had written to her, he had pointed out, politely and tactfully that this term's postal order was overdue. If all went well, her monthly letter would be arriving that week and, if it did, the postal order was sure to be enclosed.

They seized upon this ray of hope eagerly. Today was Thursday and they knew that the Headmaster was unlikely to visit the garden before the week-end. They plotted his probable movements in their minds; he would watch the cricket in the afternoons and work in his study in the evenings. Sunday afternoon was the only regular occasion on which Mr. Pemberton-Oakes was known to enjoy a stroll in his garden, and even if he did visit it before then, it was unlikely that he would include a thorough tour of the vegetable plot in his programme.

If, therefore, Aunt Angela's letter arrived on Friday or Saturday, they would have ample time to cash the postal order and restore the cucumber frame to its normal condition.

"It looks as though everything's going to be all right after all, then!" Darbishire exclaimed happily, when they had summed up their chances.

"M'yes," said Jennings, who realised the drawbacks better than his friend did. "The real trouble, of course, is that Aunt Angela's so absent-minded."

"You mean, like a professor?"

"No, she's not like a professor at all. She's . . ."

"I meant absent-minded. All profs are like that," replied Darbishire knowingly. "They do things like, say, for instance, they strike matches to see if they've blown the candle out and things like that. In fact, I heard a creasingly funny story about an absent-minded old professor who came home one stormy night and put his wet umbrella into bed and stood himself in the sink to drain." He laughed gaily at the absurdity of it; it was clear that Darbishire was already beginning to feel better.

"But Aunt Angela's nothing like that," Jennings objected. "She hasn't even *got* an umbrella—she left it on a bus last Christmas, by mistake."

"Well that proves what I said," cried Darbishire logically. "She must be absent-minded! "

"Of course she is, you ancient ruin—I told you that to start with! You don't have to prove it! The only snag is that she's so cracking absent-minded she may forget to post the letter."

"Oh, surely not—not if she likes you! My father says that the heart that is truly fond, never forgets."

"You tell your father, from me, that he's got it all wrong," said Jennings. "It's the elephant who never forgets. Gosh, I *do* wish Aunt Angela was an elephant! "

Loud footsteps approached along the corridor and the door of the tuck-box room shot open as though a small charge of dynamite had been applied to the door-knob. When Mr. Wilkins was on duty, he made no secret of the fact, and his progress round the building could be heard and followed from attic to basement. The school found this useful, for it gave them time to switch to some lawful occupation before the master on duty arrived at any particular spot, and Mr. Wilkins seldom caught an offender red-handed. This time, however, his luck was in.

"What are you two boys doing down here in the tuck-box room?" he demanded.

"We're just having a chat, sir. And then we were going to get ready for cricket," Jennings replied.

"Well, you've no business to be chatting—you're supposed to be helping to tidy the school up. There's no cricket this afternoon; everyone's got to make the place look ship-shape for tomorrow. The Headmaster has some important visitors coming."

"Yes, sir. Where shall we start ship-shaping, then, sir?" asked Darbishire.

"Classrooms and common room first," ordered Mr.

Wilkins. "Desks, lockers and shelves have all got to be turned out and all rubbish thrown away."

"Yes, sir."

The boys made for their classrooms and Mr. Wilkins' powerful voice followed them up the stairs: "And no slacking! I shall inspect the rubbish you've collected before tea, and if you haven't got plenty, I shall—I shall— well, you'd better look out."

As the boys trotted upstairs, they found everyone hard at work tidying up. The maids were washing the picture-rails, the housemen were polishing the door-knobs; Robinson was cleaning the windows, and Old Nightie had been roused from sleep at half-past four in the afternoon to dredge pellets of sodden blotting-paper from seventy-nine inkwells.

The air was heavy with the smell of floor polish, and on every landing, vacuum-cleaners whirred, brooms swept, dusters flapped and mops splashed. The Headmaster was sparing no effort to impress General Merridew's party with the spick-and-span appearance of Linbury Court School.

The classroom was a hive of activity when Jennings and Darbishire arrived. Form 3 were carrying out their orders with a will, and their efforts at spring cleaning were raising so much dust that it was difficult to see across the room.

Bromwich had prised up a loose floorboard and had collected a paper bag full of fluff and chalk dust; he wandered round the room looking for somewhere to put it, but as the waste-paper baskets were all full he had to replace his rubbish under the floorboards again. Then he went and had a few quiet words with Elmer; he apologised to him for having to tidy his tank away in the bottom of a cupboard, and promised that this state of affairs would be remedied as soon as the visitors had gone and things were back to normal. He muttered his apologies furtively, for people might think it odd if they saw him engaged in animated conversation with a goldfish.

"Come and do some work for your living!" Venables sang out as Jennings and Darbishire came through the door. "Bod and Atki and I are having a competition to see who can collect the most junk. I've got a smashing lot already and I'm keeping it in the waste-paper basket until I've got a whole heap more."

Atkinson walked by with his arms full of old newspapers and broken cardboard boxes and Venables eyed him with sudden suspicion. "Hey, Atki," he demanded, "where did you get all that?"

"I found it in the waste-paper basket," smiled Atkinson delightedly.

"But you can't have that! That's mine—I put it there," Venables protested.

"Well, if you put it in the waste-paper basket, that proves you didn't want it."

"Of course it doesn't—I put it there for safety! You ozard oik, Atki, you've been pinching my litter. Put it back, at once!"

"Well, fancy making such a fuss about rubbish. Here you are—take it, if you want it!" And Atkinson scattered the junk-pile in a wide circle at Venables' feet and skipped quickly out of range to the far end of the room.

Jennings entered the litter contest with gusto, but Darbishire preferred to scavenge alone. He made his way up and down the room on his hands and knees, spearing minute fragments of paper with a pen-nib. He was, in his imagination, a park keeper clearing up Hampstead Heath after a bank holiday.

Soon Mr. Wilkins looked in to see how the great tidying-up scheme was progressing. He had difficulty in seeing anything at all, for a choking pall of dust hung round the door, where Thompson minor had trodden on some small pieces of chalk and was now trying to fan the powdery remains towards the fireplace.

"That's enough!" called Mr. Wilkins loudly. "We'll leave this room till the dust's settled. All you boys go outside and start tidying up the quad. There's half an apple-core and a toffee-paper in the far corner. Go and pick them up—the Headmaster doesn't want his visitors to wade knee-deep in litter!"

Outside on the quad, Jennings asked: "What's all this hoo-hah in aid of, anyway? Who's coming?"

"Sir Melville Merridew," replied Temple. "The old boy who gave the Sports Cup and makes all those speeches about his schooldays being the happiest time of his life."

"Oh," said Jennings, "I thought it was royalty, at least, judging by all this flapdoodle."

"The General's a very important character," Brown explained. "He's been in the army since about the time of the Wars of the Roses, and he's been a military attaché as well. Mr. Carter says he'll probably come round and talk to us, so we'll have to be careful how we behave."

"I shouldn't know what to call him if he talks to me," said Temple. "Do I say, 'Your Worship,' or 'My Grace' or what?"

They had tidied the quad by this time and stood about wondering what to do. Darbishire, more conscientious than the others, was dusting the gymnasium bootscraper with his handkerchief. He looked up importantly as Temple's query caught his ear.

"My father's got a little book about how to address important geezers and all that sort of thing," he announced. "F'rinstance, if say, you want to write a letter to a high dignitary of the Church, you'd start off 'My Lord Bishop.' . . ."

"Yes, but he's not a bishop—he's a military attaché, whatever that is."

"I didn't think a chap could actually *be* a military attaché until Mr. Carter told me," Brown put in. "I thought they were sort of despatch case things that you carry military secrets about in."

Darbishire rose from his bootscraper and peered at his companions through spectacles thick with dust. "Oh, no," he said, "a military attaché to a foreign country is something like an ambassador and my father's book says that if you want to write to a chap like that, you end up by saying: 'I beg to remain your Excellency's most obedient servant'!"

"I should jolly well think we are," said Brown. "Look at all the orange peel and junk we've collected for him. It's enough to fill fifty military attaché cases!"

Darbishire was unwilling to let the conversation veer away from the interesting store of knowledge which he had acquired from his father.

"My father's book's got a lot more useful information about other things, too," he went on, spearing a small leaf with his nib and placing the refuse tidily in his coat pocket. "Statistics, and things like that. F'rinstance, did you know that the population of China is so big that if you put them all in a long, unbroken line and made them march day and night without stopping, it'd take twenty years for them all to go past you? It's true!" He smiled knowingly.

"How do they know?" asked Brown. "Have they tried it?"

Darbishire hadn't thought of that: it seemed unlikely, yet his father's book could not be wrong. Doubtfully he said: "Well, I suppose somebody must have done it, or they wouldn't know, would they?"

"You're bats!" said Temple. "What would happen when their shoes wore out? There wouldn't be anyone to mend them, because they'd all be marching. And they'd get a bit drowsy all that time without sleep, wouldn't they?"

Darbishire began to have grave doubts, now that his imagination was forced to picture the marching column in action. "They'd have to sleep sometimes, of course," he agreed.

"But they *couldn't*," persisted Brown earnestly, "because you said they had to march without stopping, and if they dropped out for a snooze or a snack every so often, there'd be a gap in the line."

"All right, then, perhaps there *would* be a gap."

Temple and Brown whooped with triumph. "That proves you're wrong!" they chanted. "You said the line was unbroken! Darbishire's mad! Darbishire's crazy! Darbishire's as bats as two coots!" They danced round the student of statistics, plucking imaginary straws from their hair with gestures of feigned madness.

"Ah, but what I meant was . . ." Darbishire broke off and turned to Jennings for support, but his friend was unable to give it; indeed, Jennings seemed to be in need of support himself. He stood staring before him as though in a trance, and absently tugging at a button on his jacket.

"What's up?" Darbishire inquired anxiously, and he had to repeat his query three times before his friend came to with a jerk which pulled the jacket button right off.

He led Darbishire out of earshot of the prancing madmen and said: "Listen, I've just been thinking! We haven't got till Sunday to get a new hunk of glass. If that old general's going round the school tomorrow, the Head's bound to take him into the garden—he always does with visitors."

"Oh, golly, yes, of course!" Darbishire bit his lip thoughtfully. "And there just *couldn't* be a worse time to find it all smashed than when the whole place is supposed to be looking like Buckingham Palace and he's got baronets and things in tow. Oh, gosh, why do these things always happen to us!"

"Keep calm! We've got to put our faith in Aunt Angela," Jennings reassured him. "The Archbeak probably won't have got as far as the garden till the afternoon, and if that letter comes first post tomorrow morning, I'll fox down to the village shop in break and get the beastly stuff."

"Yes, but supposing anything goes wrong?"

"It won't. Things are ozard desperate, of course, but as your father says, 'While there's life, there's hope'."

But the odds were against them, and they knew it. Supposing the village shop had no glass in stock! Supposing Mr. Wilkins kept the form in during break! Supposing the Head showed his visitors round the garden before lunch, instead of afterwards! Supposing—and this was the greatest gamble of all—supposing that Aunt Angela forgot to post that letter!

Jennings swallowed hard. "Oh, gosh," he said, "I wish I hadn't said I wished Aunt Angela was an elephant. I didn't really mean it—honestly!"

CHAPTER ELEVEN

The Visitors Arrive

THERE ARE certain days which stand out in the memory long after they have been torn from the calendar: days when hope rides high and days when disappointment lurks round every corner. To Jennings, the second Friday in July was one of these days; it was a day when the needle of Fate's barometer swung from storm to sunshine and back again with baffling swiftness. It was a red-letter day—it was a black-letter day.

It was Friday, the thirteenth!

Jennings woke early, and as soon as the rising bell sounded, he jumped out of bed and started to dress.

"What's the big rush—building on fire?" inquired Venables.

"Postman. I'm expecting a jolly important letter," replied Jennings, scrambling into his trousers. His movements were so hurried that he became entangled with his belt and had to start all over again.

Not that speed at this stage was really helpful, for even if the postman brought the expected letter, it could not be opened until Mr. Carter gave out the mail at the breakfast table; but anyone who happened to be on the spot when the postman arrived would be able to scan the envelopes —and Aunt Angela's handwriting was unmistakable.

Jennings washed and dressed and was about to leave the dormitory when Matron came into the room: "Good morning, Matron," came from five voices.

"Good morning! Best suits and clean clothes for everyone, today," she announced, "and an extra special wash

121

behind the ears. You've all got to look smart for the visitors."

"My best suit's being cleaned, Matron," Jennings reminded her. "I haven't got to get undressed again, have I?"

"Yes, of course. Clean vest, shirt and socks. You'll find them all in your locker."

Jennings tore his clothes off as fast as he could, for the postman was due any minute now. Darbishire had only reached the stage of rummaging in his locker for a missing garter when his friend again dashed to the door, weaving his arms into his jacket as he ran.

Matron called him back. "More haste, less speed," she said. "You've forgotten to put your vest on. There it is, on your chair, look."

When Jennings had dressed for the third time, he hurried down to the hall, and was just in time to see the postman cycling away down the drive and a maid disappearing into the staff-room with the letters. He told himself that it didn't really matter; he would know soon enough!

Mr. Carter sat at one end of the long dining-table glancing casually through the pile of envelopes which rested beside his plate of cereal. His movements were leisurely for he had the whole meal before him in which to attend to the post and he had every intention of finishing his breakfast first.

Half-way down the table Jennings and Darbishire sat side by side and seethed with impatience.

"Why on earth doesn't he give them out? I shall go off pop, if I don't know soon," fumed Jennings.

"I know—the suspense is unbearable," said Darbishire. "It's putting me off my breakfast. I can hardly manage this fifth hunk of bread and marmalade. It makes me go hot and cold to sit here watching him eating without a care in the world, and all the time we're waiting to know whether your Aunt Angela's memory has gone to seed, or not."

Mr. Carter finished his breakfast and strolled slowly round the dining-hall, giving out the letters. Once he stopped just behind Jennings and the boy's heart leapt with joy; but the letter was for Darbishire and Jennings clicked his teeth with exasperation.

"There's not many left now," he muttered as Mr. Carter moved away. "If he doesn't come to it soon, we've had it!"

His eyes followed the master round the room; why was he being so slow about it? Why did he keep stopping for social chats? Why . . . ? He caught his breath in excitement for Mr. Carter was approaching once again, and a moment later the precious envelope was laid on the table beside Jennings' plate.

"Oh, thank you, sir! Super-wizzo-sonic thanks!" he beamed. His eyes were shining as he clutched Darbishire by the elbow and whispered: "We're saved, Darbi! It's good old Aunt Angela all right. That's her writing as plain as the nose on your face. Yippee!"

He turned the envelope over and over, as though it were some magic formula; he was so pleased that he could not bear to let it out of his grasp. He smiled at it, and fanned himself with relief and jogged his head from side to side in sheer high spirits. "Oh boy, oh boy, oh boy! Tiddle-um-tum-tum, tiddly-pom!" he crooned.

"Hadn't you better open it?" suggested Darbishire.

"Yes, of course, but the important thing is that it's actually come. Dear old Aunt Angela—she's got a memory like an elephant, after all, bless her!"

He tore open the envelope and took out a sheet of note-paper, and the next second, his eyes opened wide in horrified bewilderment.

"Dear Mr. Tomlinson," the letter said,
"I shall be obliged if you will send me your catalogue of flowering shrubs as I have unfortunately mislaid the list which you sent me last month.
Yours faithfully,
Angela Birkinshaw (Miss)."

Jennings groaned; in a daze he passed the letter to Darbishire who read it and scratched his head in puzzled wonder. "Your aunt's bats!" he decided. "Why does she call

123

you 'Mr. Tomlinson'? Have you changed your name by deed poll or something?"

"No, that's not me—that's somebody else," Jennings explained. "I see what's happened, though. She's written two letters and got her envelopes mixed up; I've got this Tomlinson bird's letter, and he's got mine. Oh, gosh, I take back all I said about Aunt Angela not being as absent-minded as a professor."

"What a ghastly bish!" said Darbishire, as the facts became clear. "And whatever must this Mr. Tomlinson be thinking?"

Jennings snorted. "Huh! It's what *I'm* thinking that matters. Never mind about Mr. Tomlinson—*he's* all right! At least he jolly well ought to be; dash it all, Darbi, he's got my fifty pence!"

The deduction was correct. At the very moment that Jennings was bemoaning his fate, Mr. A. Tomlinson, *Nurseryman & Seedsman*, was standing in his suburban shop, pondering over a letter which had arrived by the morning post.

"Dear John," it began,
"I am sending you a postal order for fifty pence, which I expect will come in useful at the tuck-shop."

There followed three pages of good advice and news of Cousin Wilfred's white rabbits, and the letter was signed, "Your affectionate Aunt, Angela."

Mr. Tomlinson was surprised. He had not known that he had an Aunt Angela, and in any case his name was Albert, not John. However, fifty pence was fifty pence, so he slipped the postal order into his waistcoat pocket and whistled gaily as he opened the shop.

During morning break, a grey Rolls Royce purred quietly up the drive and came to rest outside the front door. From the car jumped a small boy wearing a green pullover and corduroy trousers, and he was followed a moment later by an attractive young woman, with blue eyes and fair hair.

Then, from the driver's seat stepped Lieut.-General Sir Melville Merridew, Bart., D.S.O., M.C.

"This is the old place, Diana," he said to his daughter-in-law. "Changed quite a bit from my time, of course, but if it was good enough for me and good enough for his father, it ought to be good enough for Roger, eh!"

General Merridew was tall, thin and very upright, with snowy hair and bushy eyebrows; the points of his handlebar moustache were just visible to anyone standing directly behind him.

The Headmaster received his guests in the drawing-room. The General, he knew well, but he had not met the seven-year-old Roger and his mother before.

"So this is the young man, is it?" He smiled down at the General's grandson and extended his hand, but the boy quickly slipped his hands behind his back and stepped away out of range. He had not met any headmasters before, and he was taking no chances.

"Shake hands, Roger," urged his mother. "This is the Headmaster."

"Huh!" grunted Roger, not impressed. In point of fact he was bitterly disappointed. From all he had heard of these high-ranking humans, he had imagined that a headmaster must be about eight feet tall and dressed like a commissionaire outside a luxury cinema. Mr. Pemberton-Oakes was tall, but he was not eight feet; his suit was well-cut, but it was not a crimson uniform with gold buttons. Why, the man hadn't even a row of medals across his chest!

"I can whistle through the gap in my front teeth," Roger told him proudly. "I bet you can't!"

The Headmaster smiled and changed the topic of conversation. It was clear that the child had never been subjected to boarding-school discipline. Never mind—he would learn!

Mr. Pemberton-Oakes was proud of his school as he showed his visitors round that morning. The linoleum glistened and the brass door-knobs shone. Whenever they entered a classroom, a dozen boys with gleaming pink faces and well-brushed hair stood up smartly; no button was missing from any jacket, no sock hung limply round any ankle.

Even in Form 1 classroom, all ties were neatly knotted under the chin and not beneath the left ear as was their usual custom. Binns had spent twenty-five minutes polishing his shoes with his bath towel, and he edged his feet forward hoping that the visitors would notice the result. But he kept his hands behind his back, because his fingernails had absorbed nearly as much polish as his shoes.

Form 3 classroom was exceptionally tidy, for the havoc of the boys' spring cleaning had been put right later by the domestic staff. Jennings had disciplined a zig-zag parting into his hair, and although Friday was not his usual polishing day, Darbishire had cleaned his spectacles specially in honour of the occasion.

Both boys stood politely at ease when the party entered, and no one could have dreamed of the despair that filled their minds at the thought that a visit to the garden was high up on the list of the visitors' engagements.

"This is our third form," announced the Headmaster in so genial a voice that Venables had to look twice to see who was speaking.

"Splendid, splendid—fine body of lads, Headmaster; they do you credit!" said the General, who was deeply impressed by everything he saw. An orderly routine of obeying orders and jumping to it smartly was just the thing his grandson needed to knock the rough corners off him. "Well, Roger, how would you like to come to school here, eh?" he demanded.

"Huh!" said Roger, and scowled at the bright shining faces of Form 3 with distaste.

Mrs. Merridew did not say, "Huh!" but she shared her son's doubts to some extent. Her own childhood had been spent in a boarding school where freedom was almost unknown, and it was this memory that made her keen to find a school for Roger where he would be able to enjoy him-

self in happy surroundings, free from the repressive atmosphere which had cast such a pall of gloom over her own
schooldays. So far, all she had seen had confirmed her
worst suspicions; Roger would never be happy in this
formal, parade-ground of a place, where hair was so
smartly brushed and shoes shone like mirrors. If she could
have seen the boys under normal conditions, she would
have known that things were not always like this but, as it
was, Diana Merridew could not imagine these straight rows
of tailors' dummies throwing off the shackles of dignified
behaviour and enjoying themselves in a rousing rough-and-
tumble.

She was wrong, of course—hopelessly wrong; and the
pity of it was that Mr. Pemberton-Oakes had arranged this
unnatural exhibition of highly-polished cherubs specially
to please her!

The conducted tour of the building went without a hitch;
the visitors were shown the oak-panelled library, the system
of overhead ventilation in the dormitories, the patent, self-
closing boot-lockers, the thermostatically-controlled dish-
washer in the kitchen and the up-to-date, tiled bathrooms
with heated towel-rails. They heard about the proud record
of scholarships and the health-giving properties of the
sandy sub-soil on which the school was built.

General Merridew was delighted with everything, but,
as the tour proceeded his daughter-in-law became more
and more convinced that Linbury Court was not the place
for Roger. To judge from Mr. Pemberton-Oakes' remarks,
his boys seemed to spend their free time in admiring the
scenery and meditating deeply. This, his mother knew,
would not suit Roger, who would be far happier making
mud-pies out of the sandy sub-soil than in strolling quietly
about on it without getting his shoes dirty.

It was a pity, too, that in the process of tidying up, all
the things which Mrs. Merridew was looking for had been
put away. One glance at the hobbies' room on a normal
day would have shown her that the boys' out-of-school
interests were well catered for; too well, perhaps, for floor
and shelves would have been stacked high with model air-

craft, puppet theatres, wireless sets, stamp albums, photographic equipment and shapeless pieces of leather and clay waiting to be coaxed into the likeness of home-made wallets and tea-pot stands. But now, these objects had all been locked out of sight in the cupboards, and the hobbies' room looked as bare and uninviting as a bus shelter.

The school was remarkably quiet during luncheon. The boys knew they had to be on their best behaviour and although the strain was severe, they kept their voices down to a polite hum and only occasionally spoke with their mouths full. The Headmaster was proud of them; the General was pleased with them; but Mrs. Merridew was secretly appalled that seventy-nine boys could be so lacking in spirit.

"The old General looks jolly pleased about something," said Atkinson as he tucked into his pudding. "Hope he asks for a half-holiday!"

Venables cast a furtive glance at the top table where the guests were sitting.

"I expect he will, if he's in a decent mood," he replied. "When I'm a famous Old Boy in about a hundred years' time I shall come back here three times a week and kick up a hoo-hah if they don't give a half-holiday every time I ask for one."

"You won't!" said Darbishire, from across the table. "You may *think* you will when you're young, but when you get past a certain age, you go bats. All grown-ups do; it's called, er—something like sea-lion."

"Sea-lion?" echoed Atkinson. "Gosh, I never knew that before. I suppose it's because they grow those walrus moustaches."

"No, it's not sea-lion, it's . . ." Darbishire struggled to remember the word. "Senile, that's it! It means that when you're about thirty-five or so your brain starts to pack up and you go as bats as two coots. I've often noticed it!"

Venables stole another glance at General Merridew who was beaming with pleasure at some story that the Headmaster was telling him. "I reckon you're right," he said. "After all, you wouldn't sit next to the Archbeako and still go on looking as pleased as a dog with two tails unless there was something the matter with you. I expect the poor old codger's been sea-lion for years! " He shook his head sadly and took another mouthful of prunes and custard.

"I can't imagine an old geezer like that ever being a boy at school," pondered Atkinson. "He must have been here round about Queen Boadicea's time, I should think."

"He must have been young once," Darbishire pointed out. "Like all the chaps in those ancient school photos they've got in the attic. My father's in one of those—he was at school here years ago and I laughed like a drain when I saw his photo. He's wearing an Eton collar and one of those suits with a waistcoast and . . ."

Darbishire found his left arm clutched in a vice-like grip. Jennings, who had scarcely spoken since the meal started was clutching his friend's sleeve, while his eyes flashed with the inspiration of genius. Darbishire stared in alarm; this sort of behaviour was likely to attract attention from the top table.

"What's the matter, Jen?" he asked. "Swallowed a prune?"

"Listen, Darbi, I've got a supersonic idea," his friend answered in a breathless whisper. "It's about the cucumber frame. I can't tell you now, because it's a top priority secret, but directly after lunch, we'll nip up to the attic and you'll see what I mean."

Luncheon took rather longer than usual that day, and it was further drawn out by the Headmaster's suggestion that the school would be deeply honoured if its most distinguished Old Boy would care to say a few words. General Merridew enjoyed making speeches and for twenty-five minutes he stood up and repeated, almost word for word, the same speech he had made on Sports Day the previous term. The boys listened patiently, for they knew the speech almost as well as the General did and they knew, too, that if it ran true to form, it would end up with a request for a half-holiday.

Their hopes were fulfilled, the half-holiday was granted and at two o'clock, seventy-seven boys filed quietly out of the dining-hall and prepared for a long afternoon of cricket, photography and similar summer term pastimes.

The seventy-eighth and seventy-ninth boys, however, made straight for the attic. Jennings' plan was simple and he explained it to Darbishire as they pounded up the stairs.

"It was you talking about the old school photos that gave me the wheeze," he said. "Nobody ever looks at them now and the glass on one of those frames would just about fit over the cucumbers."

"Gosh, yes, massive idea! Saved at the eleventh hour!" Darbishire slapped his friend on the back and danced merrily up the stairs behind him.

Every year since 1875 the school had assembled for the annual photograph to be taken. The more recent ones were ranged in rows round the walls of the common room, but there was no space for the accumulation of three-quarters of a century, and each year as the new photograph was hung up, an old was taken down and stored in the attic.

There was no one about when Jennings and Darbishire reached the top landing, but caution was necessary if they were to carry out their plan undetected. They would have to hurry, too, for the Headmaster's party had headed for the cricket field after lunch and in twenty minutes or so they would probably be making their way towards the garden.

Darbishire pressed the latch and the attic door opened with a piercing squeak.

" 'Ssh!" said Jennings sternly.

"It's no good saying ' 'Ssh'!" complained Darbishire. "It's the door that needs oiling, not me."

He led the way inside and stood blinking in the dusty gloom. There was a small skylight in the sloping roof and it allowed enough daylight to pass through for Darbishire to take in his surroundings.

The attic was full; there were broken beds and old desks and scenery from long-forgotten school plays. There was a magic lantern with tarnished brass fittings and a case of butterflies standing on a stack of out-of-date wall maps. There were surprising things too; useless, broken junk which it was difficult to imagine ever having been used in a boys' school—a perambulator, a parrot cage and a pair of ballet shoes.

The old photographs were in a far corner; some were hanging on the wall and others were stacked in heaps on the floor. Darbishire picked his way towards them. "It's pretty ghostly in here, isn't it?" he prattled. "I bet there's lots of mice about!"

Jennings had not heard for he was still on the landing, making sure that no one was about. He came in and the door closed squeakily behind him. "All clear! Let's get on with the job quickly," he said.

Darbishire sniffed and strained his ears; he was sure the place was overrun with mice for there was a strong mousey smell in the air. Perhaps they could catch one and keep it as a pet. "Listen," he whispered, "I thought I heard one, then, didn't you?"

"Didn't I what?"

"Didn't you hear it squeaking?"

"Of course I did," returned Jennings impatiently. "I'm not deaf, but we can't do anything about it if we haven't got an oil-can."

His friend stared at him in surprise. "You're bats! You can't stop mice squeaking with an oil-can!"

"Who said anything about mice? I'm talking about that wretched door. It'll give us away, if we're not careful."

"Well, I was talking about the mice and you said . . ." Darbishire lapsed into sudden silence at the sight of Jennings' warning gestures.

" 'Ssh!" he breathed. "We've got to keep quiet; Mr. Hind's room's just underneath here, don't forget. Now, let's get on with the job!"

Soon they found a frame which looked about the right size. Jennings lifted it from the wall, whipped out his pen-knife and slit the brown paper pasted round the edge of the frame. Then he removed the cardboard-backing and eased the glass away from the photograph.

"There you are," he said triumphantly. "Hang on to the glass while I put my knife away."

He glanced at the yellowing picture in his hands and smiled. There were about sixty boys in the photograph and, to Jennings, their old-fashioned school uniform looked as odd as fancy dress. The smaller boys had long black stockings over their knees, while the seniors wore cycling knickerbockers, black bow ties and waistcoats which buttoned high over their chests.

The staff looked even more peculiar; a matron and a master's wife had skirts reaching to the ground and huge hats which blotted out the faces of the boys in the row behind him. The masters wore mortar-boards and high stiff collars; beards and side-whiskers grew in profusion.

Linbury Court School, Summer Term, 1905, was printed underneath the photograph in faded ink letters.

"Come and have a look at this, Darbi," said Jennings. "This is what you'd have looked like if you'd been here in your great-grandfather's time. Don't they look rare! Look at this funny old geezer in a white waistcoat and a watch-chain!"

For a moment they forgot the urgency of their errand and giggled quietly at the absurdity of school uniform at the beginning of the century. Then, Jennings said suddenly: "Here, what are we laughing at! We've got no time to hang about. I'll carry the glass and you go ahead and see if the coast's clear."

Darbishire tiptoed to the door and paused with his finger on the latch. "This dust's getting into my eyes and nose and everywhere," he whispered thickly. "I think I'm going to sneeze."

"You can't sneeze now; Mr. Hind might hear," Jennings protested in an undertone.

"I can't help it. I've got a tickle." Darbishire wrinkled his nose and blinked his eyes in a desperate effort to stave off the impending explosion. "Ah . . . ah . . . ah . . . !" he panted.

"Shush!" urged Jennings.

"Yes, I will in a minute, but first of all I've got to ah . . . ah . . . as-shoosh!"

It was a loud sneeze, as sneezes go, and the noise rang

round the attic like a trumpet blast. A broken vase on the magic lantern vibrated in sympathy with the high-pitched note and echoed the sound like a distant air-raid siren.

The two boys stood stock still and listened. Had Mr. Hind heard? Apparently not, for everything was quiet on the landing below and after a few seconds Darbishire ventured down the stairs to survey the route.

He stopped on the landing and beckoned to his friend to join him. Then he did the same thing on the next flight of stairs and in this fashion the boys descended to the main hall. The going was more difficult on the ground floor for there were blind corners to hamper them, but they managed well enough. Jennings crouched in doorways with the precious glass while Darbishire scouted ahead and looked cautiously round each bend.

"Come on; no one about," he called back over his shoulder and Jennings left cover and started on the next stretch of corridor past the library. He had gone half the distance when Darbishire, who was peering round the next corner, suddenly waved his arms in a desperate signal to retreat.

"Get back!" he breathed hoarsely. "Someone's coming! ... It's ... it's ... Oh, golly!"

CHAPTER TWELVE

Shortage of Glass

JENNINGS LOOKED round for somewhere to hide, but even as he did so he knew that it was hopeless. He was in open country and there was no time to go back.

As he stood undecided, Mr. Carter's voice sounded from round the bend of the corridor. "Well, Darbishire! Are you practising semaphore or merely waving a fond farewell?" And the next moment the master had turned the corner and his eye was on Jennings.

It is difficult to appear calm and collected when one is carrying a suspicious-looking object, but Jennings did his best. He smiled and said: "Good-afternoon, sir. Jolly decent of the General to ask for a half-holiday wasn't it, sir?"

Mr. Carter was looking at the pane of glass and his mind was seeking some explanation. "What have you got there?" he asked, "a portable windscreen?"

"No, sir. Just a piece of glass, sir."

"I can see that. Rather a dusty piece, too."

"Yes, sir." Jennings found the conversation difficult to sustain. He looked down at the glass as though surprised to find that he was carrying it. "Yes, it is rather dusty, sir, when you come to look at it. It might be a good idea if I cleaned it, don't you think, sir?"

"Why, Jennings?"

"Well, sir . . ." *Why?* What on earth could he say? "Well, sir, then you'd be able to see through it better, sir."

Mr. Carter waited for further explanation and Jennings floundered on: "You see, it's just a piece of glass which wasn't doing much good where it was, so Darbishire and I

134

thought we'd go and try and find somewhere where it'd be more use, if you see what I mean, sir."

Then, surprisingly, Mr. Carter said: "Run along, then, Jennings. Er—no don't run or you'll drop it. Walk along very carefully."

He watched the boys till they were out of sight. This must be part of the plan which they had been so busy discussing the other day, he decided. Now, what on earth could they be up to? Clearly, they were on their way to carry out some urgent repair work, but—and here, Mr. Carter furrowed his brow in deep concentration—wherever had they found that pane of glass? He could have asked them outright, of course, but he had a fancy for letting things work themselves out to their logical conclusion. He could afford to wait. He knew, from experience, that he would find out the details sooner or later.

As they slipped out through the side door, Darbishire turned to his companion with a little, nervous laugh.

"Phew, what a bish!" he said. "Fancy running *slap-bang-doyng* into Mr. Carter like that. You don't think he suspected anything, do you?"

"No, of course not. He probably thought we were just, er——" Jennings searched his mind for some good reason to excuse their odd behaviour. "Well, there's no actual school rule that says you can't walk along the corridor carrying a hunk of glass, is there?"

"Perhaps not, but he must have thought it funny."

"I didn't hear him laughing."

"I mean the whole thing must have looked fishy. My father says that you should never . . ."

"Don't natter, Darbi. We're engaged on a super-important secret mission and we don't want to get cluttered up with your father's famous proverbs."

Away to their left the cricket field was dotted with magenta-and-white blazers as the school settled down to enjoy the half-holiday, and in the distance Jennings caught sight of the Headmaster's visitors emerging from the cricket pavilion. So far, so good; masters and boys were well out of the way, but there was no time to lose, for the

135

conducted tour would be almost certain to make for the garden as soon as their inspection of the pavilion was over.

The boys hurried to the gap in the hedge and crawled through. The pane hindered their progress to some extent and Jennings breathed a sigh of relief as he stood safely inside the garden with the glass still intact. Everything seemed very quiet now, and the afternoon sunshine bathed the garden in an atmosphere of peace and stillness.

Jennings found himself speaking in a whisper: "I say, isn't it lovely in here—so peaceful and picture-skew!"

"Esque," Darbishire corrected in a low voice.

"What did you say?"

"I said you mean picture*esque*, not picture-*skew*."

"Have it your own way," Jennings answered. "There's no point in arguing about what sort of picture it is. After all, it's picture *frame* that we've got to worry about." He led the way along the path to where the cucumbers were ripening in the warm July sun.

First of all they picked up the broken fragments of the middle pane and laid them on the path. Then Jennings laid the new piece in position. It fitted well enough; if anything it was rather on the large side, but a small overlap on to the neighbouring panes was not likely to be noticed at a casual glance. He surveyed his handiwork proudly. "Looks fine, doesn't it, Darbi!"

"Smashing," his friend agreed. "It almost fits like a glove!"

"I'm not trying to make it fit like a glove," Jennings reminded him. "All I want to do is to give it a nice new pane."

"Tell it to eat green apples, then—that'll give it a nice pain," Darbishire replied facetiously. He was feeling so relieved at the successful outcome of their plan that a wave of lightheartedness swept over him and he shook with subdued laughter at his little pun.

Jennings looked at him in shocked surprise. "What are you laughing at?"

"I'm laughing at me," gasped Darbishire through cackles

of delight. "I made a joke. You said: 'Give it a pane' and I said . . ."

His friend snorted in disgust. "Oh, *that*! That's not funny. That's the feeble sort of joke that Binns and all that crush in Form 1 would make. Pull yourself together, man; we've got to clear up the broken bits and get out of here pronto."

"Sorry, Jen," replied the humorist humbly and started gathering the fragments into his handkerchief.

There was a potting-shed near at hand, so they carried the remnants of the broken glass inside and hid them behind a row of flower-pots. That was that! There would be just time to escape through the hedge if they went at once. Jennings dusted his fingers on his handkerchief and stepped outside.

The next second he was back in the shed again and pulling Darbishire down into the cover afforded by a large wheelbarrow. One glance along the path had told him that escape was out of the question; the General and the Headmaster were approaching. Already they had passed the rose garden, and they were heading straight towards the cucumbers.

Jennings groaned inwardly; if only he had been out in the open he would have seen them coming while there was still time to slip back to the hedge; but they had spent nearly two minutes in the potting shed and now their escape route had been cut off.

"What's the matter?" asked Darbishire.

"Archbeako and party—heading this way at forty knots. They won't come in here, though; we'll just have to lie doggo till they beetle off."

The situation was awkward, though not dangerous. At all events the main part of their scheme had been carried through, and a cucumber frame complete in every detail awaited the party's inspection.

A few moments later the sound of voices drifted into the potting shed and footsteps came to rest a short distance along the path.

". . . now if only you could have seen the garden in

137

April, General—the daffodils were a picture." The voice was the Headmaster's and it sounded uncomfortably close. "If you'll stand over here, you'll be able to see the laburnum trees to better advantage."

Jennings fixed his eye to a chink in the wall; General Merridew and his host were standing together beside the cucumber frame. Mrs. Merridew and her son were at the far end of the garden looking at the lily-pond and were making no effort to catch up with the others. Jennings took cover again as the General's deep tones boomed out in reply.

"Yes, very fine display, Pemberton-Oakes! This garden was always a picture in July, you know. I can remember the school photo being taken on this very spot, the first summer term I was here. Must be almost seventy years ago —round about 1906. Let me see, I should be able to remember. Long time ago . . . it must have been, er— um . . ." There was a short pause while the Old Boy searched his memory; then he went on: "No, I'm wrong! It must have been 1905."

"Really! Well before my time, I'm afraid," replied the Headmaster.

The General heaved a sigh. He had enjoyed an excellent lunch, and now these familiar scenes of his childhood were giving him a feeling of homesickness for the vanished days of childhood. How it all came back to him! He could remember that photograph being taken as though it had happened yesterday; he had been wearing his first Eton suit and he had sat in the front row between old "Tubby" Tickner and "Tadpole" Fitzarchway. What had become of them? He had hardly given them a thought since leaving school, but now they came flooding back into his mind with such freshness and vigour that it seemed as though Time had rolled back almost three-quarters of a century in the space of a moment.

His eye was moist as he turned to his host and said: "I suppose that old photo was thrown on the rubbish heap years ago. Pity! I'd give a lot to be able to see that old group once again!"

"I can help you there," said the Headmaster, eager to please his guest. "We've got every photograph right back to the very first one. Very quaint, some of them. Ha-ha-ha! When we've finished our little tour of the garden we'll join Mrs. Merridew and Roger and then I can take you up to the attic and show you. 1905 you said, didn't you?"

"Oh, I hardly like to trouble you all that much, merely to satisfy an old man's passing whim."

"Not at all, not at all! I shall be only too pleased!"

Inside the potting-shed Jennings and Darbishire stared at each other in dismay. This new development was going to lead to more trouble if something were not done about it very quickly. It was bitterly disappointing, for until this moment everything had gone surprisingly well. Jennings opened his mouth to speak and then shut it quickly as the conversation outside started again.

"What wonderful gladioli, Headmaster! . . . And what's in this frame—cucumbers?"

"Yes, they're coming along nicely, aren't they! H'm, that's funny!" Mr. Pemberton-Oakes leant forward and examined the middle pane closely; there was dust on the glass and the marks of small fingers. Now, what did that mean? Surely no boy could have . . . ! The half-formed suspicion slipped from his mind as he turned his attention to what his guest was saying.

"Bit near the cricket field for a cucumber frame, isn't it? Wouldn't do to have any balls sailing over the hedge, eh what!"

"Oh, no! The boys don't play cricket near my garden," the Headmaster assured him. Then he took another look at the cucumber frame and he wasn't so sure!

"I suppose there's be a terrible row if they did, eh! Ha-ha-ha——!" The General threw back his head and laughed heartily. "I remember once in 1906 I was knocking a cricket ball about with old 'Pongo' Bannerdale—he became an archdeacon, you know—and he sent down a long-hop and I hit it clean through the window of the head-master's study. Ha-ha-ha! What about that, eh! Clean through! Ha-ha-ha!"

Mr. Pemberton-Oakes joined in the hilarity. "Dear me, how diverting!" he laughed. "Ah, well, boys will be boys! It must have made a deep impression on you, General, if you still remember it after all these years."

"It made an even deeper impression on the window-pane, eh, what! Ha-ha-ha!" The General was in an excellent mood and his deep laugh pealed merrily through the still afternoon air.

Then the laughter faded and the footsteps died away as the two men strolled on to a distant part of the garden.

Jennings looked at Darbishire and shook his head in perplexity. He was surprised at Mr. Pemberton-Oakes joining in his guest's laughter. But his shock at this flippancy was nothing compared with his horror at the thought of what was going to happen next. Within a matter of minutes, the party would be heading towards the attic to inspect the 1905 school group. Every photograph from the school's foundation until recent times would be there, with one glaring exception. They would find a gap on the wall, the picture-frame balancing on top of the magic lantern, the cardboard backing tossed untidily on to the perambulator and the very photograph which they had come to see resting between the bars of the parrot cage like toast in a toast rack. The human brain reeled at the thought of what would follow when this unhappy state of affairs was investigated at a later date.

"Come on, Darbi, quick. If we hurry we may just have time," said Jennings in an urgent whisper.

"What are we going to do?"

"There's only one thing we *can* do. If they make a bee-line for the attic, they've wizard well got to find that photo in one piece when they get there. We shall have to take the glass off the cucumbers and beetle back with it. We may just do it, if we run."

The visitors had passed out of sight and the coast was clear as far as the gap in the hedge. Stealthily the boys crept out of the potting shed and started to put the emergency plan into operation.

"Oh, gosh, what a hoo-hah!" lamented Darbishire.

"Supposing they decide to have another look at the cucumbers afterwards—we can't keep running backwards and forwards all afternoon with the same hunk of glass."

"We'll have to risk that. Anyway, there'll be an ozard sight worse hoo-hah if we don't get this glass back on the photo before they get there." He lifted the pane carefully and together they made their way back through the hedge.

Darbishire opened the side door leading to the hall. "Talk about a bish!" he observed bitterly. "D'you think the Head will get into a bate if he finds out?"

"Well, of course he will—he's bound to!"

"But he went off laughing like a drain about the old boy busting a window in the olden days."

"Maybe he did, but if anyone busts one in the 1970's, he doesn't think it funny at all. It just goes to prove what you said about grown-ups going sea-lion—they don't seem to understand things clearly after a certain age."

Darbishire scouted ahead and returned to say that the way past the library was clear of spectators. "I think I know why grown-ups carry on like that," he remarked as they started the next lap of the journey. "My father says 'Time heals all wounds' and as it's about seventy years ago since the old boy . . ."

"Huh!" snorted Jennings. "If your father thinks I'm going to cart this slab of glass backwards and forwards for seventy years till the wound's healed . . ."

The library door opened and Mr. Carter walked out.

"Hello!" he said, "still taking pieces of glass for an airing?"

"I—er, well, sir . . ." Jennings stopped. After all, what was there to say?

Mr. Carter looked at him curiously and observed: "You certainly think up some odd hobbies to occupy your free time. You'll have to come and take my french window for a breather when you've nothing better to do!"

By this time he had a shrewd idea of what was afoot. Later in the day, when the guests had departed, he would go into the matter in detail, but for the moment he decided to say no more. He returned and walked off down the corridor, leaving the boys guessing as to how much he knew; his back was towards them so they could not see the quiet smile which played round the corners of his mouth.

"Come on," said Jennings as the master turned the corner. "Ozard bad luck meeting him a second time, but I still don't think he suspected anything."

They mounted the stairs and hurried into the attic. Jennings said: "Ssh!" as the door squeaked open, but now it was a race against time and speed was even more important than secrecy.

Darbishire retrieved the photograph from the parrot cage while Jennings slipped the glass back into the frame. The backing was the difficult part for there were little nails set into the wooden frame at intervals, and these had to be bent forward to hold the cardboard in place. The nails were rusty and kept breaking off and they wasted precious minutes trying to bend them into position. They even took down some of the other pictures and tried to borrow some nails from them; but nothing would work properly, and the only result was that three unframed photographs were now spread out over the floor instead of one.

"This is ghastly!" said Darbishire as the last nail snapped off and failure became inevitable. "What are we going to do? They'll be here in a minute. I wish we hadn't done this! My father says that . . ."

He broke off and listened. Footsteps were ascending the stairs and a voice was speaking.

"Only a few more stairs, General—we're nearly there," said the voice and a moment later the latch clicked, the attic door opened with an ear-splitting screech, and M. W. B. Pemberton-Oakes, Esq., M.A. (Oxon.), ushered his distinguished guests into the room.

CHAPTER THIRTEEN

The Difficult Guest

FOR A MOMENT the Headmaster was too surprised to speak; then, icily he demanded: "What are you two boys doing in here?"

And though there was a perfectly good answer to this question, Jennings did not know where to begin. Should he start with the absent-mindedness of Aunt Angela, the sentimental yearnings of General Merridew or with Darbishire's only straight ball in the England v. Australia Test Match?

"We—er, well you see, sir, what actually happened was . . ." he began, but Mr. Pemberton-Oakes was not prepared to spend the entire afternoon in the attic and he broke in sharply.

"Don't prevaricate, Jennings. I demand a straightforward answer to a simple question. What were you doing when I came in?"

"I was putting a piece of glass in this picture-frame, sir."

The Headmaster glanced at the repair work spread out over the floor and jumped to the only conclusion which seemed to fit the facts. It was the wrong conclusion, but it was some days before he found *that* out.

"I see," he said slowly. "Yes, I consider that is a very creditable way of spending your leisure." And turning to his guests he went on: "These boys, instead of wasting their half-holiday in idle pursuits, have elected to repair the old school photographs as their good deed for the day."

The General smiled approvingly: Roger said, "Huh! " and Mrs. Merridew thought what a pity it was that the boys were encouraged to grope about in dim-lit attics instead of enjoying themselves in the glorious sunshine.

"Very good of them," nodded the General. "I'm glad to think there's somebody who doesn't consider it too much trouble to keep the Old Boys' photos in a decent state of repair." He gave the Headmaster a reproachful look, for he felt rather hurt that these historic photographs should be stored in a junk-filled garret, while the more recent ones occupied places of honour on the common-room walls.

Jennings' conscience woke up and prodded him into a second attempt to confess, but the Headmaster cut him short. "Of course, General, I always encourage the boys to spend their half-holidays in some useful and instructive manner," he said. "The odd-job man keeps a supply of glass handy for repairs of this kind but"—and a note of genuine surprise crept into his voice—"I must say, I hardly expected a couple of third form boys to think of asking him for some, specially for this purpose."

The two picture-repairers looked down at their shoes with becoming modesty. They would have to own up afterwards, of course, but it would hardly be fair to spoil the Headmaster's pride in their handiwork while his guests were still present.

Mrs. Merridew looked at the boys with sympathy. "Poor little fellows," she thought. "They're so repressed that they can't help looking guilty even when they're caught doing good deeds by stealth. This sort of place would never suit Roger!"

The Headmaster turned to the wall behind him. "Now, let me see, General, which was the photograph you particularly wanted to see?"

Darbishire picked it up from the floor and said: "Here it is, sir. This is the 1905 photo that we've been putting the glass on."

The Headmaster wheeled round and his eyebrows rose in astonishment. "And however did you know, Darbishire, which one it is that the General wishes to see?"

Darbishire shifted nervously from one foot to the other; he opened his mouth, but no words came. Fortunately, the General opened *his* mouth at the same time and a torrent

144

of "Well, well, well's" and "Bless my soul's" rang round the room as the Old Boy seized the photograph and gazed at it fondly. "There I am, in the front row in my very first Eton suit—just as I thought!"

He held the picture under the skylight and looked at it for a long time without speaking. It was a sacred moment for General Merridew and no one liked to disturb his wistful memories of a by-gone age. After a full minute had passed he turned away from the skylight and his voice was unsteady with emotion as he said: "Well, well, well! How this old photo takes me back!" Then he blew his nose very loudly.

"Let me see, grandad," demanded Roger and climbed up on an old wash-stand and peered over the Old Boy's shoulder. "Golly, grandad, you do look funny—you haven't even got a moustache!"

The General was smiling again now and excitedly picking out his colleagues from the group. "By jove, here's Old 'Pie-face' Pottinger in the second row," he exclaimed. "He's doddering about in a bath chair, now. And bless me, if this isn't Old 'Bonehead' Blatterweather! I wonder what became of him?"

"You'd better run along, now," the Headmaster told Jennings and Darbishire, for he feared that the General's reminiscences might last some time. Mrs. Merridew thought the same, for she asked: "Do you think they might take Roger with them? He's getting rather bored, trailing round with us."

"Yes, yes, of course!" the Headmaster agreed. "You'd like to meet some of the boys, wouldn't you, Roger?"

"No," said Roger.

"But you'll have to get to know them if you come to school here, won't you?"

"I don't want to come to school here. I don't like this place. I think it's horrid!"

"Now, now, Roger," said his mother.

"Well, so it is! They've all got clean knees and I bet they're not allowed to climb trees and get in a mess. That's what *I* like doing!" he finished up proudly.

"Oh, but I'm sure you'll like *these* boys," persisted the Headmaster, favouring Jennings and Darbishire with a smile. They smirked back, secretly amazed that the Headmaster was capable of such affectionate feelings. They had never suspected this before, and even now they ascribed most of it to his efforts to humour a difficult child.

"I'd better introduce you, hadn't I?" the Headmaster went on. "This is Jennings, Roger; and this is Darbishire."

"How d'you do!" said Jennings and Darbishire.

"Huh!" said Roger.

Then they were introduced to Mrs. Merridew and the General; and Darbishire, who remembered what his father's book had said about ceremonial forms of address, replied to the Old Boy's greeting by saying that he begged to remain his lordship's most obedient servant.

"Take Roger round the school and show him the things that will be of interest to him," said Mr. Pemberton-Oakes. "Show him the books in the library, the scholarship honours boards, the collection of sports trophies and, ah, perhaps the tuck-shop, eh! Ha-ha!"

As the three boys left the attic, they could hear the General starting on what promised to be a long anecdote of his schooldays.

"Seeing old 'Bonehead' Blatterweather in this photo reminds me of the time in 1907 when the bishop came to tea and left his hat in the hall." His deep, resonant voice followed them down the stairs. "Well, old Blatterweather put the bishop's hat on, just for a joke; and danced around in it. Suddenly, he looked up and there was the bishop and the Headmaster watching him from the top of the stairs . . ."

The boys were out of earshot by now, and though Jennings would dearly have liked to know what had happened to Blatterweather, he thought it wiser not to loiter. Roger followed them, rather unwillingly, and as he did not seem disposed to talk, Darbishire turned to Jennings and said: "Phew! That was a bit of luck, wasn't it? I thought there was going to be the most hectic rumpus, and he was actually pleased with us!"

146

"Yes, but what fools we were not thinking of it before," Jennings replied.

"What! Mending all those old photo frames in our free time? No jolly thanks!"

"No, you prehistoric ruin! Why didn't we think of the odd-job man? If we'd gone to Old Pyjams and asked him for a chunk of glass it would have saved all that wear and tear on our nerves."

"Well, we still need some, don't we?"

"Yes, and the sooner the better. Look, Darbi, you take Roger and show him the tuck-shop and everything and I'll go and find Old Pyjams, and if he's feeling decent and gives me a bit, I'll fox into the garden and fix it right away."

"Right-o," his friend agreed. "See you later, then. Come on, Roger—I expect you'd like to see the scholarship honours board first, wouldn't you?"

"No," said Roger decisively.

Jennings found Robinson in the boiler-room. Yes, he *had* got some glass, he admitted, but that didn't mean to say that he was willing to give away panes as freely as handbills. "Glass costs money, glass does," he said. "Those panes don't grow on trees, you know!"

"No, I didn't think they did," replied Jennings and wondered what a glass-leaved tree would look like. "But it's super urgent, Py—er, Robinson, really it is, and I could pay for it later on when I get some more money."

Grudgingly, Robinson agreed and led the way to the cupboard in the carpenter's shop where the glass was stored. Jennings selected a suitable piece and took his leave, murmuring voluble thanks as he went.

He clutched the new pane to his chest and hummed gaily as he started off along the corridor. Considering the narrow escapes they had had, it was amazing how well things were turning out, he thought. It would be the work of a moment to slip into the garden unobserved and . . . His humming broke off in the middle of a note as Mr. Carter walked round the corner.

"You know, Jennings, this is getting monotonous," the master observed. "Every time I walk past the library, I meet you carrying a pane of glass."

Jennings agreed that it was a remarkable coincidence.

"This is the third piece in half an hour," Mr. Carter went on. "You haven't smashed three cucumber frames, have you?"

Cucumber frames! So Mr. Carter knew about it!

Jennings looked uncomfortable and said: "Oh, no, sir. We only broke one, really, but we've had to do a sort of shuttle service because of the shortage of glass, sir. Er— how did you find out, sir?"

"I put two and two together," replied Mr. Carter, "and they added up to Jennings and Darbishire continuing to play cricket near the Head's garden after they'd been told to move farther away."

"Oh! . . . Yes, sir. I'm very sorry, sir. I suppose there'll be an awful row, now you know, sir."

Mr. Carter thought for a moment before replying. "You know, Jennings, I should have been less inclined to take drastic action if you'd told me about it when it happened."

"I wish I had, sir! The trouble we've been to—you wouldn't believe it, sir! It's been more hair-raising than any punishment."

"Why didn't you own up in the first place, then?"

"Because of getting evening cricket stopped for the whole school, sir. P'r'aps if it'd been anyone else, the Head might have let them off, sir, but I've been in a lot of trouble lately, sir, and I didn't want everyone to be punished again, just because of me."

Mr. Carter took a less serious view of the matter when he realised what had prompted Jennings' unusual conduct. The damage would have to be paid for, naturally, but the boy had had so many punishments lately that Mr. Carter saw no point in giving him any more unless it was going to teach him the error of his ways. Good conduct, after all, was an attitude of mind, rather than blind obedience to a list of rules, and as punishment did not seem to work very well in Jennings' case, perhaps a reward for virtue would have more effect.

"Well, Jennings," he said slowly, "all I can suggest is that you make a determined effort to behave like a civilised human being. I shall put you on probation until this time tomorrow when I shall see the Headmaster and discuss the matter with him. That means you've got just twenty-four hours in which to pull your socks up . . . No, no, you silly boy—I didn't mean it literally. Leave your socks alone when I'm talking to you. You've got until this time to-morrow in which to convince me and all the other masters that you are really trying. Understand?"

"Yes, sir. Thanks very much, sir. I'll try all right, sir. Honestly I will."

"Good. Now you'd better put that glass on the cucumber frame and then go out to the cricket field."

"Oh, but I can't, sir. The Head's just told me and Darbishire—er Darbishire and I . . ."

"Darbishire and *me*," corrected Mr. Carter.

"Yes, sir; he's told us to take this new boy round and show him everything."

"He told *you* and *Darbishire* to do that?"

"Yes, sir."

Mr. Carter blinked in surprise. What on earth was Mr. Pemberton-Oakes thinking about? He had seventy-nine boys in his school and he had to pick Jennings and Darbishire, of all people, for a task which required skilful handling. Roger Merridew was a "difficult" child and quite unused to doing what he was told—so much Mr. Carter remembered from the Headmaster's remarks earlier in the week. Surely, then, it would have been better for him to be shown round by some reliable prefect!

Doubtfully, he said: "I see. Well, now you've got a chance to do something useful, Jennings, so mind you do it properly. When you're on probation for your conduct, we take a keen interest in how you carry out little jobs of this sort."

"Yes, sir. Thank you, sir."

Jennings walked on, his mind brooding on what his

149

housemaster had said. "On probation" meant that he was being given another chance, and by a stroke of good fortune he had just been given a task in which he could prove his worth. He would look after this Roger Merridew as a mother hen tends her favourite chick; he would spare no effort to interest and entertain him. No one should say that J. C. T. Jennings had been entrusted with an important mission and had failed to make the grade.

He felt happier and just a little proud as he placed the glass on the cucumber frame—quite openly this time, for he had Mr. Carter's permission. Then he returned to the building to look for Darbishire and Roger Merridew.

He found them in the library. First of all he saw Darbishire standing helplessly in the middle of the room and gazing into space with a look of glassy despair.

"Where's this Roger chap you're supposed to be looking after?" Jennings asked.

Darbishire pointed to the top of a bookcase and Jennings caught his breath in surprise. Roger Merridew was crawling along some ten feet above the ground and eyeing the space between one bookcase and the next in an expert manner. "He's going round the room without touching the floor," Darbishire explained.

"But he can't do that here—not in the *library*!"

"I've told him, but he won't take any notice of me. He says he can go round his bedroom like that in thirty seconds and he thinks this room's easier because he'll be able to swing on the curtain rod when he gets to the bay window."

"Gosh!" Jennings was appalled. Given the right time and place, he was as keen as anyone on this particular feat of gymnastics, and indeed, he held the Dormitory 4 record for the anti-clockwise "off the floor" circuit. But here in the library, where the furniture was polished oak and treasured silver cups gleamed on the mantelpiece, such a thing was out of the question. Besides, someone might come in at any moment and catch them!

"Hey, Roger, come down at once! You're not allowed up there!" Jennings called.

150

"Huh!" replied the shrill voice from somewhere near the ceiling. "I'm not afraid, even if you are! D'you want to make something of it?"

"Do I want to make something of *what*?"

"I don't know. It's a thing I heard a chap say on the telly. Sounds good, doesn't it!" He narrowed his eyes and repeated the phrase from the side of his mouth. "Want to make something of it—huh?"

"I think it's a sort of challenge," said Darbishire. "He's insulted you and he wants to know whether you're going to fight him about it."

"He's crackers! I'm supposed to be looking after him —not bashing him up," snorted Jennings. "Come down here, at once, Roger, or I'll . . ."

"You'll bash me up?" inquired Roger hopefully.

"No, I'll . . ."

But at that moment Roger missed his footing in trying to leap from one bookcase to the next; he landed softly on a leather couch, but the shock had unnerved him and he opened his mouth and screamed at the top of his voice.

"'Ssh! For goodness' sake—'ssh!" Jennings urged. "You'll have everyone beetling in to see what the row's about." And sure enough, the library door opened a few seconds later and an anxious inquirer popped his head into the room.

It was Atkinson. "What's up? Place on fire, or ship sinking?" he asked.

"Neither."

"What's the air-raid siren for, then?"

"It's all right," Jennings explained. "We're just showing this chap round. The Head told us to look after him."

"Well, he didn't tell you to start torturing the poor little thing the moment his back was turned, did he? Dash it all, Jen, he's only half your size!"

"We never even touched him! We couldn't have got near enough if we'd wanted to," protested Darbishire.

"No? Sounded as though you were killing a pig. Still, it's not my business." And Atkinson wandered off to fetch his batting-gloves from the tuck-box room.

151

Roger was quiet again now and Jennings decided to take a firm stand. "Now you've got to come round with us and look at everything we tell you to," he said. "We'll start here. This is the library . . ."

"I've told him that," said Darbishire.

". . . and these are all the books on the shelves."

"I can see that," said Roger. "You might as well say, this is the floor we're walking on, and up there's the ceiling."

Jennings ignored the tone of the small boy's remarks. It was clear that he had never been to school or he would not have been so outspoken to his seniors. Ah, well, he would learn! Jennings held him firmly by the elbow and propelled him through the door.

"Now, out here in the corridor, we keep the honours boards," the guide explained. "Now, if say, supposing you won a scholarship we'd bung your name up there on the wall. That'd be nice, wouldn't it?"

"Huh! You can keep your old boards," said Roger. "I'm not going to look at them and you can't make me." He shut his eyes tight. "Want to make something of that?"

Jennings shrugged his shoulders. "This is hopeless, Darbi! Still, we'll have to go through with it, because the Head's sure to ask us if we've shown him important things, like this."

"I can't see it! I've got my eyes shut!" squeaked Roger triumphantly.

"Well, you can jolly well listen while I read it all out. It'll serve you right, for not trying to be decent." Jennings' patience was wearing thin, but he set about his task with quiet determination and read aloud:

"1875 R. K. Blenkinsop, scholarship to Repton . . .
1877 G. H. Johnson, scholarship to Marlborough . . .
1878 C. L. N. Herbert-Jones, scholarship to Winchester . . .
1880 . . ."

Roger's loud yawn drowned the next name on the list. "How much more is there?" he asked.

"Just about a hundred years! . . . 1881 B. A. Dadds, scholarship to Harrow . . ."

"I can't wait all that time—I shall be older than Grandad."

"Well, if you open your eyes and look for yourself I shan't have to read them all out."

"Huh!" said Roger, but he opened his eyes all the same. Then he said: "It's a waste of time showing me all these old things, because I can't read long words like that."

"Haven't you ever been to school?" asked Darbishire.

"No, but Mummy's teaching me, and I've got a reading book. I've got up to page seven. '*Dan is a man*'," he quoted by heart. " ' *Dan ran with a pan. The fat nag has a rag in a bag. Dan has a nap in the gap. A bad lad had . . .*' "

"All right, all right," said Jennings hastily. "I can see you're a jolly fine reader when you like, but we haven't got time for any more."

"What are we going to do, then—something nice?" asked Roger eagerly.

"Yes, of course. We'll go and look at the boot-lockers. That'll be super, won't it?"

"Huh! Is that all you can think of to do? This rotten old place is a washout, if you want to know what I think!"

There was nothing really wrong with Roger: nothing that a few weeks amongst boys of his own age would not put right; but as an only child, brought up without playmates, he expected to have his own way without the slightest regard for anyone else's feelings. School was a disappointment to him, and trudging round behind his elders had become a bore.

Jennings and Darbishire did their best to entertain him. They told him about Mr. Wilkins' geometry lessons, and the Headmaster's Latin class; they explained how many bad conduct stripes were needed for an afternoon's detention; they told him he must not run in the corridors or walk about with his hands in his pockets; they told him that he would have three baths a week and that his fingernails would be inspected before every meal; they told him when he must be silent and when he would be allowed to talk. In short, they did their best to prepare him for a normal school life, but the more they said, the more rebellious their guest became.

As they left the main building and wandered together towards the cricket field, Roger asked: "Don't you *ever* do anything nice at school? As far as I can see you spend all day reading dreary old books and washing your hands."

Darbishire hastened to correct this impression. "Well, we *did* have a super smashing thing we used to do, but it got stopped last Monday," he said. "We used to build huts near that pond over there." And he pointed towards the wood, past the cricket field.

"It was supersonic," Jennings added. "Our hut was easily the best, because Darbishire's a famous inventor, you know. You should have seen all the gadgets he made. You'd be surprised!"

"What's a gadget?" demanded Roger, showing some interest at last.

"Well, like, say, for instance, pieces of string so's you can open the front door without bothering to stand up, and an ear-trumpet so you can chat with anyone who happens to be on the roof." And Jennings painted an exciting word-picture of a squatter's life in the hut-colony before the ban was imposed. He spoke fondly of the ventilating-shaft-cum-periscope; he dwelt on the joys of having an emergency drinking supply which could also be used as a patent fire-extinguisher; he added a few words in support of yacht clubs and pontoon-suspension bridges and touched on the delights of hut-warming parties when sardine and walnut cake were on the menu.

As the tale was unfolded, Roger gradually lost his sullen look and became more and more excited. Open-mouthed and round-eyed, he listened to the things that could be done in a community of squatters, and for the first time that day he felt that here was something worth looking into!

"You say you have feeds in these huts?" he gasped with delight. "Oh, goody, goody, goody! Come on, let's go over there and have one now!"

"We can't; they're out of bounds," Darbishire pointed

out, and as this phrase was obviously new to Roger, he translated: "We're not allowed to go there, and in any case our hut's just a busted ruin, because the Head got jammed in the back-room boys' department, and started lashing out."

"We'll go and mend it, then," suggested Roger, to whom school rules meant less than nothing. "And if no one's allowed over there, that's all the better 'cos there won't be anyone there to see us. Come on!" And he danced impatiently along the footpath.

"No, we're not going," said Jennings firmly, though he would very much have liked to fall in with Roger's suggestion; after all, they had been told to show their guest everything. On the other hand, it was also their duty to see that he behaved himself, and as he was the type of child who caused havoc in libraries, what on earth would he get up to if he were let loose in the untamed jungle beyond the suspension bridge?

"Come along; we're going back," decided Jennings and he and Darbishire turned and led the way towards the quad. They had gone some distance before they realised that their guest was not following hard behind them. Jennings glanced over his shoulder and then wheeled round and faced along the way they had come. "Hey, stop! Come back here!" he shouted.

But Roger Merridew had a clear start of fifty yards and was streaking towards the wood as fast as his short legs would carry him. If those huts were anything like as good as they sounded, they would be well worth a visit, he thought.

CHAPTER FOURTEEN

Hue and Cry

SCIENTISTS tell us that the human brain is like a com-
mander-in-chief's headquarters during the course of a
battle. From reports which reach his control-room, he
builds up a picture of what is happening, weighs up the
chances of this plan and that, and sends his orders to the
battle-front.

So it was in the control-room of Jennings' mind as he
watched Roger Merridew running full tilt towards the
pond. Eyes flashed a message to brain: *Enemy heading
nor'-nor'-west at 6 m.p.h.* it ran. *Am keeping him under
observation. Over!*

Quick as thought, the order was transmitted from brain
to legs: *Take up action stations for pursuit of enemy,
identified as R. Merridew. Proceed with caution: combat
area known to be dangerous territory.*

Translated into human action this meant that Jennings
took a quick glance round and then started to run. Reinforcements arrived—consisting of Darbishire—and the task
force pounded forward after its quarry.

"We've no business to be going after him—there'll be a
frantic blitz if we're copped out of bounds," panted Darbishire as he ran.

"Well, we can't just do nothing! Suppose he gets lost or
something—what then? You are a bazooka, Darbi, telling
him about the huts and calmly pointing out where they
were."

"How was I to know he'd do a bunk? Anyway, we were
told to tell him everything and we'd be failing in our duty

156

as his lordship's most obedient servants if we hadn't. My father says . . . Phew! Not so fast!" and the Rev. Percival Darbishire's gem of wisdom dissolved into gaspings and blowings as his son struggled to keep up the pace.

When they reached the wood, they caught a brief glimpse of Roger leaping across the wobbling struts of the suspension bridge, but by the time the boys had reached the spot, their quarry had disappeared amongst the huts.

Jennings called as loudly as he dared: "Roger, come out! We're not allowed over here!"

There was no answer and Jennings called again, but his plea fell upon deaf ears. Roger Merridew had gone to earth in Venables' low-built tunnel of a hut and he was looking forward to the most exciting game of hide-and-seek which he had had for some time.

"It's no good, Darbi. We'll have to go over the bridge and rout him out," said Jennings.

"But it's out of bounds! The Head said so; no one's allowed over the bridge because it's out of bounds! He put it out of bounds last . . ."

"All right, all right, I *know*! You don't have to go on saying it's out of bounds a hundred and fifty thousand times an hour! Anyway, if we can catch him fairly quickly we'll be able to get back before anyone finds out. It should be all right," Jennings went on, "because at least we know the Head won't be coming over here . . . At least, I shouldn't think so . . . At least, I hope not!"

All the same, Jennings was worried. Mr. Carter had given him twenty-four hours in which to prove himself a reliable member of the community. Not more than thirty minutes of this time had passed and already he was breaking bounds and had lost a new boy entrusted to his care. And if he didn't find the wretched child very soon . . . ! He swallowed hard. Imagination boggled at what Mr. Carter and the Head would have to say about it!

Jennings led the way across the suspension bridge and the hunt started in earnest. Darbishire scoured the district round the edge of the pond, while his companion moved slowly forward searching the undergrowth on the higher ground.

But it was ideal country for a fugitive and Roger had the time of his life. He crept from hut to hut, taking cover behind the thick clumps of bulrushes, always on the move, always ready to double back on his tracks if his pursuers should draw near.

There were false alarms, too. Darbishire heard a rustling in the reeds and plunged after the sound only to find two moorhens enjoying the afternoon sunshine. He scowled at them, for the ground was soft and his legs were now muddy from knee to ankle. "Silly little birds!" he said crossly, but the moorhens took the scolding very well. It was almost as though the fifty-three Spanish galleons were getting their own back for the indignities of the previous Sunday!

So far, the pursuers had made no effort to go about their task warily. Indeed, they kept announcing their whereabouts with frequent appeals to Roger to come out of hiding—appeals which grew more desperate as time went on. Finally, Jennings approached his partner with a new plan of campaign.

"We're just wasting our time, calling to him," he said. "And until we know roughly where he is, it's like looking for a needle in a haystack. I vote we lie doggo and wait till he gives himself away."

"Okay," Darbishire agreed. They were standing by Atkinson's tall, thin hut, so they slipped inside and stood quiet and alert.

Roger was disappointed when the sounds of the chase were suddenly hushed. It had been great fun, wriggling on his stomach through the long grass and crawling in and out of the huts. Once Darbishire had passed so near that Roger could have touched him, but a thicket of reeds had screened him from view and Darbishire had wandered by with his eyes straining straight ahead.

There had been few playmates in Roger Merridew's life and he was determined to make the most of a first-class game of hide-and-seek while he had the chance. There was no malice in his heart, no spite in his thoughts. It never entered his head that this exciting game could result in endless trouble for his guides.

He could hear nothing now. Had they gone away and left him to play alone? He rose to his knees and peered round; still no sound, still no one in sight. He stood up and skipped lightheartedly towards the pond.

Jennings saw him first; through a spyhole he had made in Atkinson's hut, he caught a glimpse of a green pullover and grey corduroy shorts making for the water's edge. He waited until the figure came nearer; then with a shout of "Come on, Darbi, quick!" he dashed out of the hut and raced away in pursuit.

Roger squealed with joy. So they *were* still playing after all! He took to his heels and dashed helter-skelter through a soggy swamp on the bank of the pond, splashing mud freely in all directions. On he ran without troubling to look where he was going, and a moment later, he tripped and fell headlong into a thicket of briars and brambles. Frantically, he struggled to his feet and dragged himself clear, leaving a portion of grey shirt and strands of green pullover behind him. As he pelted away, a six-inch gash showed in the seat of his curduroy trousers.

Jennings was gaining on him and Roger leapt at the first spot of cover he could see. It was the entrance to Bromwich's semi-basement elephant trap, and he slithered blindly down the slope and rolled over and over on the earthy floor at the bottom.

The chase was over. Kindly, but firmly, Jennings helped the captive to his feet and escorted him up to ground level as Darbishire came dashing up to join the fray.

"Have you got him? Oh, wizzo!" he shouted, and then stopped and stared at the small boy in wide-eyed dismay. "Oh, golly, just look at him!"

Roger Merridew was not a pretty sight. He was mud-splashed from head to foot and thin red scratches ran down his arms and appeared again above the socks drooping about his ankles. The least observant spectator could tell that the child's clothes had lost something of their newness; shirt, shorts, pullover, socks, shoes—all carried evidence of his headlong flight through swamp and bramble.

Darbishire looked away. The sight was too much for him. Roger, on the other hand, was not interested in his appearance; he was beginning to take a fancy to these two boys who were doing so much to entertain him.

"Jolly decent game, isn't it!" he squeaked happily. "I was pretending I was an aeroplane."

"But look at your shoes!" lamented Darbishire. "They're wringing wet!"

Roger glanced down at his feet. "Well, let's pretend I was a seaplane, then, and I had to pancake on the water."

"Oh, golly, whatever are we going to do?" Darbishire wailed "I've never seen anyone in such a mess—except you last Sunday, Jen."

"Never mind about me," returned Jennings. "We've got to get this chap spruced up a bit before the Head starts looking for him." He pondered for a moment and then said: "Look, Darbi, if we smuggle him up to the bathroom, and bung him under the shower, I could take his clothes outside and give them a good brush."

"Yes, but they're torn! We can't sew them up without thimbles and bodkins and things, and if we go to the sewing-room, there's bound to be a hoo-hah!"

"Well, let's get away from here, for a start. We don't want to be copped out of bounds."

In gloomy silence they made for the suspension bridge; only Roger was unconcerned. "It's all right," he told them. "I often get as dirty as this at home. Mummy won't mind a bit."

"Maybe your mummy won't, but our Headmaster *will*," Jennings replied. "Look at that great tear in your trousers!"

"That doesn't matter, either. I've got lots more pairs at home. I've got a blue pair and a green pair and a brown pair and a grey pair with white checks and . . ."

"I don't care if you've got fifty million pairs at home! I don't care if they've got yellow spots and red, white and blue stripes! What I want to know is, whatever's the Head going to say when he sees you looking like a second-hand scarecrow?"

Darbishire touched his friend lightly on the arm. "You'll soon know, Jennings," he said in a flat, resigned voice. "He's zooming down on us for a roof-level attack!"

Jennings glanced across the bridge. Sure enough, three people were approaching from the direction of the cricket field. They were—reading from left to right—Lieut.-General Sir Melville Merridew, Mrs. Diana Merridew and M. W. B. Pemberton-Oakes, Esq.

Several things had happened during the previous hour which caused the Headmaster to wear a grim and forbidding expression as he led his guests towards the pond. The first one had been Atkinson's fault, and there was no excuse for it whatever.

Atkinson had not gone straight back to the cricket field after collecting his batting-gloves. The ear-splitting shrieks which had attracted his eager footsteps to the library had not been repeated, but he had hung around for fear of missing any further excitement.

He was disappointed, for the next time he had passed along the corridor he had found Jennings patiently reading the scholarship honours board aloud, while Roger listened with his eyes tight shut. Then they had moved off and Atkinson could think of nothing better to do than to resume his interrupted game of cricket.

He was crossing the main hall on his way out when he noticed a black homburg hat, and suddenly he felt an overwhelming desire to try it on. He knew that it belonged to the General and this added zest to his craving. The urge grew stronger, so, after a furtive look round, he tiptoed to the hall table, picked up the hat and placed it on his head.

It was a pity, he thought, that none of his friends was there to witness this daring act of bravado, but at any rate he would be able to boast for weeks to come that he had actually done something which no one else—except, of course, the General—had ever had the nerve to do.

The hat was too large for Atkinson; it came well down

over his eyes and made his ears stick out like small pink wings. Greatly daring, he skipped across the hall to admire his reflection in a mirror, and while he was in the very act of making faces at himself in the glass, he heard a sound which made his heart leap and his blood run cold.

It was a loud bellow, and it came from the top of the stairs behind him. Scarlet with embarrassment, Atkinson wheeled round and snatched the hat from his head. He was, of course, too late, for there, staring down at him were the Headmaster and General Merridew.

The bellow was repeated and, to his amazement, Atkinson realised that the General, far from being angry, was roaring with laughter.

"Ha-ha-ha!" he laughed as he came down the stairs. "Old 'Bonehead' Blatterweather to the life! Caught in the act, just like old 'Bonehead' and the bishop, eh, what!"

"Precisely," agreed the Headmaster. His feelings were mixed. Politeness to an honoured guest urged him to indulge the General's sense of humour, but on the other hand, he was extremely annoyed with Atkinson for taking such an inexcusable liberty. The Headmaster did his best; with his right eye he tried to freeze Atkinson with an icy stare, while his left eye lit up in lively appreciation of the General's joke. The strain on his facial muscles was considerable.

"Well, well, well!" the General went on genially. "What a coincidence! Takes me right back to 1907. The bishop's hat was a black one, too. Rather like mine except that it had strings on it."

He dabbed his mirth-damped eyes on his handkerchief while Atkinson stood first on one foot and then on the other, his mind reeling with bewilderment. He had done something frightful, and he could not understand what the joke was. Why did the General think his name was Blatterweather? Who was "Bonehead"? What had 1907 got to do with it? Where did the string-hatted bishop come in?

Atkinson gave it up and, mumbling profuse apologies, he replaced the hat on the hall table and was allowed to escape.

Diana Merridew had watched the little comedy and had said nothing. She was mildly amused at Atkinson, and a little worried at the Headmaster's disapproval. Knowing Roger as well as she did, she could foresee that Mr. Pemberton-Oakes was going to have quite a busy time registering disapproval if ever her son became a boarder. Her depression deepened as they made their way to the study where tea awaited them.

"Now, I think you've seen everything," said Mr. Pemberton-Oakes, "so it only remains for me to tell you something of our methods here at Linbury. By means of small classes, we maintain a very high standard of academic work and promising boys are always coached for scholarships." He felt that he was talking rather like the school prospectus, so he went on in less formal tones: "Tell me, Mrs. Merridew, would you say that Roger is a studious boy, by nature?"

Mrs. Merridew thought of Roger's reading lessons and shook her head. *Dan is a man* could hardly be described as a high standard of scholarship.

"Work isn't everything," said the General. "I always came bottom of the form when I was here. What young Roger needs is firm discipline with no nonsense, to learn to play the game and to take a pride in his appearance. I remember a poem I learnt years ago—I forget how it goes, but it sums it all up neatly. I expect you know the one I mean."

"You need have no fear on that score," the Headmaster answered. "Our discipline here is based upon mutual respect and we are most particular about personal tidiness." He waved his hand towards the window through which a group of boys could be seen playing cricket. "Take any one of those boys," he invited generously, "and you'll find him smartly turned out with a spick-and-span neatness which will stand comparison with any school in the country."

"Yes, I'm sure it would!" said Mrs. Merridew.

The General rose to his feet. "There's a breathless hush

163

in the—er, there's a breathless hush, *somewhere*," he declaimed, waving his tea-cup in the air.

"I beg your pardon?" queried the Headmaster, out of his depth.

"I think my father-in-law means it's very quiet in here," interpreted Mrs. Merridew.

"No, no, I don't, Diana," said the General. "I was trying to remember that poem:

> " 'There's a breathless hush in the close, tonight,
> Ten to make and the match to win,
> A bumping pitch and a . . .'

something or other, and then it goes on to say, 'Play up, play up! and play the game!' That's what I was trying to think of; and the second verse starts off . . ."

Mrs. Merridew knew that the General would be prepared to recite ill-remembered verses of poetry until dark unless something were done about it, so she rose and said: "Thank you so much for showing us round, Mr. Pemberton-Oakes. It's very kind of you to have taken all this trouble."

"Not at all," smiled the Headmaster, "and if you could let me know fairly soon whether Roger is to come here in the autumn, I shall be happy to make all the necessary arrangements."

"I can tell you that now," she answered.

"Splendid! You'd like me to enter him for next term?"

"No, I'm afraid not."

General Merridew nearly dropped his tea-cup. "Eh, what's that, Diana?" he barked. "You . . . you're not going to send him?"

Mrs. Merridew shook her head.

"But, dash it all, Diana—why ever not? Very fine prep school—Linbury. And as smart a body of lads as you could hope to meet in a month of Sundays. Bless my soul, I don't understand this at all! If it was good enough for me it ought to be good enough for a young scamp like Roger."

"It's not that," Mrs. Merridew replied quietly. "If anything, it's the other way about; Roger isn't good enough for Linbury, if goodness means changing him into a highly-polished little boy with smartly-knotted bootlaces."

"Oh, but really, I hardly think . . ." the Headmaster began, and then fell silent, uncertain what his guest really meant.

"Please don't be offended," she went on. "But, you see, I went through all this business of being polished till I shone when I was a girl. Where I went to school, we were never allowed to behave naturally, and we loathed it. And I decided that any son of mine should have a chance to grow up in happy surroundings where he could enjoy a certain amount of freedom. I admit everything here is organised most efficiently, but from what I've seen, the boys aren't given much chance to be themselves." She hated saying it, and she felt worse when she saw that Mr. Pemberton-Oakes was hurt by her remarks, but after all, she must be free to decide important things like this for herself.

The Headmaster was not so much hurt, as stunned! Surely one did not have to look far to see signs of freedom and self-expression: the hobbies room, for instance, containing every device from puppetry to percussion bands: or the hut colony, where the boys had, until lately, been encouraged to express themselves in a dozen different forms of art and craft.

But there was no point in listing these activities, for Mrs. Merridew had seen no sign of them. Too late, the Headmaster decided that he had stressed the wrong things and shown his guests a school which was too good to be true. The best suits, the close haircuts, the unbelievable tidiness of everything had been a mistake. Perhaps Mr. Carter had been right after all; perhaps it would have been better if the school had been wearing its normal "lived-in" appearance.

General Merridew was as disappointed as the Headmaster, but he could not persuade his daughter-in-law to change her mind. "Pity!" he murmured. "A great pity. I'd set my heart on the boy coming here. That would have made three generations of Merridews who were proud to have spent their earliest schooldays in the old place. However, it's up to you, Diana, and if you feel like that about it, there's no more to be said. We'd better go and find Roger and get back to town."

They all strove hard to make casual conversation as they left the study, but the polite chat sounded rather forced. The Headmaster was distressed to think that his school was not considered suitable for the grandson of its most distinguished Old Boy; and Mrs. Merridrew felt uncomfortable in her mind, for she knew what a blow her decision was to the two men.

When they reached the quad, the Headmaster beckoned to Bromwich who was coming in from the cricket field. Bromwich wondered what was coming. Had Elmer been discovered in the classroom cupboard? Apparently all was well for the Headmaster said: "I want you to find Jennings and Darbishire for me. Tell them to bring Roger Merridew to the hall."

"Yes, sir." And Bromwich made off again towards the cricket field.

"Bromwich!" The Headmaster called him back. "You are not likely to find them out of doors. I imagine that they will be somewhere in the building."

"Oh, but, sir, I know where they are! I saw them about twenty minutes ago and they were running . . ." He stopped abruptly, conscious that he had said too much.

"Well, go on, Bromwich! In which direction were they going?"

Bromwich bit his lip in an agony of indecision. He had thought it odd at the time that Jennings and Darbishire should be heading for the prohibited area as fast as they could run; and if he now blurted out this information, the Headmaster might think it odd, too. But one cannot stand mute for ever and finally he was obliged to say: "Well, sir, I thought I saw them going towards the pond, sir."

"The pond! But surely, I made it quite clear that . . . ! All right, Bromwich—you may go. I will attend to this."

And turning to his guests the Headmaster explained: "There seems to have been a slight—ah—misunderstanding. If you would care to walk over with me, we shall probably meet the boys returning."

Thus it was that, glancing across the suspension bridge, Jennings caught sight of the three persons whom he least wanted to see at that particular moment. The Headmaster, for his part, did not seem particularly pleased when he saw Jennings; but when he caught sight of Roger Merridew, he was speechless.

"Well—I . . . Good gracious! . . . Bless my——! Words fail me!" he said, when speech returned. "Jennings and Darbishire, come here at once!"

They came. Slowly and hopelessly they crossed the suspension bridge and ranged themselves before the Headmaster, while Roger danced behind them waving happily to his mother.

Mr. Pemberton-Oakes looked at them with that expressionless face which always denoted trouble of the worst possible kind. Then he said: "I have never, in the course of my professional career, known anything to equal this flagrant act of disobedience. I entrusted this boy to your care. Why, therefore, you have taken him out of bounds and allowed him to get into this dishevelled condition, I am at a loss to understand." He paused for an explanation.

"We were just trying to be his lordship's most obedient servants, sir," Darbishire began, but Jennings interrupted. "We're very sorry, but we couldn't really help it, sir. Roger wanted to come over here, and we said he couldn't, and he said . . ."

"That's quite enough, Jennings," replied the Headmaster. "I really cannot believe that two boys of your age could be forced to come here against your will by a small boy some three years your junior and scarcely more than half your size."

"Oh, but, sir, you don't understand . . ." But the Headmaster had turned away and was apologising to Mrs. Merridew in a dozen different positions. "I'm most terribly sorry this has happened," he assured her. "An occurrence of this sort is very rare here, believe me, and I shall see to it that the culprits are severely dealt with."

"Please don't apologise," Mrs. Merridew answered. "Roger doesn't look any the worse for it; in fact he's beginning to look more like his usual self."

"I'm all right, Mummy," Roger broke in. "I like this school now, 'cos these boys have been playing hide-and-seek with me. It was ever so exciting and we've all had a lovely time! "

The remark was made in all innocence but to the Headmaster it could mean only one thing. Sternly he ordered Jennings and Darbishire back to school with instructions to report to his study after breakfast the next morning.

As they walked across the cricket field, the high-pitched squeak of Roger's merry prattle faded behind them. "Listen to him! " groaned Darbishire. "It's all very well for him—he's enjoying it! He hasn't got a hectic blitz coming to him after breakfast tomorrow! I don't know what the young people of today are coming to! I'm sure we never carried on like that when we were young—well, younger than we are now, anyway! "

"You're quite right," Jennings agreed. "You see things differently when you get old. Take this afternoon, for instance; all that rushing about has put years on me." He sighed deeply. "Any more hoo-hahs like that and I'll be as sea-lion as two coots by the time I'm grown up! "

CHAPTER FIFTEEN

Mr. Wilkins Hits a Six

It was a perfect summer morning. The dew sparkled on the close-mown turf of the cricket square and the sun, still low in the east, shone from a cloudless blue sky. It was early, and the dormitories were still draped in a pall of sleep as Old Nightie, the night-watchman, emerged from the gloomy depths of the stoke-hold and plodded flat-footedly on to the quad to sniff the soft morning air.

It smelt good to him after the choking fumes which hung, thick as fog, around the boiler. He took a heavy silver watch from his waistcoat pocket, saw that it was one minute to seven and trundled off to the electric bellpress to rouse the sleeping school to the glories of another day.

There were five sleepers in Dormitory 4, and three-fifths of them awoke to the summons of the rising bell with joy in their hearts and a song on their lips. The song was tersely criticised by the remaining two-fifths who were feeling neither joyous nor musical.

"Put a sock in it, for Pete's sake!" complained Jennings, as the top notes of Venables' piercing soprano invited all nymphs and shepherds within earshot to come away. "It's all very well for you to lie there singing the top of your head off. You wouldn't feel so jolly pleased with yourself if you'd got to stop one of the Archbeako's rockets after breakfast."

Dormitory 4 had heard the sad story of Roger Merri-dew's visit to the pond, and they sympathised.

"After all, it wasn't your fault, Jen," Temple pointed out. He threw back the bedclothes and tried to pick his shirt up from the floor with the toes of his left foot. "Just tell the Head that the chap did a bunk and you had to follow him."

"I told him that yesterday and he didn't believe it because he said Darbi and I were twice the size of that chap, put together."

"He didn't mean if Roger was put together—he meant if *we* were," Darbishire explained. "Or rather as we were both twice his size, we ought to have stopped him because we'd have been four times as big, if we were put together, if you see what I mean."

Nobody did, and Venables said: "You're bats! If you and Jen were put together you'd hardly be able to move, let alone run four times as fast. But I still don't see why this chap wanted to run away from you, anyway. He must have been crazy! "

"Oh, yes, he is! " Atkinson sounded quite definite on this point. "I happen to know it runs in his family. I expect he's caught it from his grandfather, because he's as crackers as two cuckoos."

"What—old General Merridew! How do you know?" asked Temple.

Atkinson lowered his voice to a confidential undertone. "Well, yesterday afternoon, he thought I was a chap called Blatterweather and he said he hadn't got any strings on his hat."

"Who hadn't—Blatterweather?"

"No, the General. He got the date wrong, too. He kept thinking it was 1897. I couldn't understand all he was talking about, but the poor chap was raving like a coot."

Dormitory 4 sounded interested in this odd behaviour and pressed for details.

"Well, I happened to be in the hall . . ." Atkinson paused; on second thoughts it would be embarrassing to confess that he had been caught red-handed wearing the distinguished visitor's hat. "And—and, well, that's all, really. He just came downstairs and started having these delusions."

His room-mates nodded in understanding. The man was obviously senile.

The conversation rambled on, but Jennings was too much upset to listen. It was not the thought of punishment that worried him, but something far more serious. He had failed the Headmaster and had let the school down badly in the presence of visitors. Obviously, he reasoned, Roger Merridew was to have come to Linbury as a new boy, but now, thanks to that wretched business by the pond, his mother was bound to have changed her mind.

He put this aspect of the matter to Darbishire as they stood cleaning their teeth by the washbasins. "Now, supposing you were this chap's mother, Darbi, and . . ."

"I'm not," Darbishire objected, foaming at the mouth with pink toothpaste, "and what's more, I never shall be!"

"Maybe not, but look at it from her point of view. If Roger was your son, what would you do?"

"I'd keep very quiet about it, and try and pretend he wasn't," Darbishire decided. "And if that didn't work, I'd never let him out of my sight, unless I went with him."

"Don't be so feeble, Darbi! What I mean is, supposing you were going to send him to school here, because you'd heard Linbury was a pretty decent sort of a joint, as schools go, and then, when you got here, something happened like —well, you know!"

His friend nodded. There was no avoiding the fact that if Roger was sent to some other seat of learning, the blame would be placed at their door.

"Why does it always have to be *us* that these things happen to?" complained Darbishire. "There are seventy-nine chaps in this school, and they have to go and choose us to take charge of that slippery little Roger, just because we happened to be in the attic."

"It goes farther back than that," said Jennings. "It goes right back to when we had that hut-warming party with Ven and Bod and they agreed what a good wheeze it'd be to make a home-made yacht."

"That's right! If they hadn't been so keen to sail it at

171

once, you'd never have fallen in and then the huts wouldn't have been out of bounds yesterday."

"Yes, and on top of that, they wouldn't let us play cricket in their net, so we just *had* to play our Test Match bang slap next to the Head's garden; so if anyone was to blame for that direct hit on the cuke frame, it was Bod and Ven!"

Darbishire was shocked at such villainy. "Gosh, what rotters they are. Doing all that and then expecting us to take the blame for it! Let's go and tell them what rotten cads they are, shall we?"

"Yes, all right." But even as they wheeled round from the basins they realised the uselessness of such wild reproaches, and changed their minds. In their heart of hearts they knew that no amount of righteous indignation would shift the blame from where it really lay.

Jennings and Darbishire were very quiet during breakfast and though their friends tried hard to cheer them up, the shadow of the Headmaster's study seemed to lie across every mouthful of fried bread and tomatoes.

It would be of little use for them to protest their sorrow, for the damage was already done and the Headmaster, not knowing Roger as well as they did, would dismiss their explanation as an unworthy evasion of responsibility.

At five minutes to nine, the two boys set off for the study. They were accompanied part of the way by a small crowd of well-wishers and sympathisers who trooped behind like a funeral procession, uttering words of doubtful comfort.

"D'you think they'll get a swishing?" asked Atkinson.

"Oh, they're bound to," said Bromwich. "What a pity it's the summer term. If it was winter they'd be wearing thick underpants."

Binns on the fringe of the group provided realistic sound-effects of the Headmaster's cane in action. "Pheew-doyng! . . . Pheew-doyng!" he squeaked, but the others silenced him abruptly.

"Buzz off, Binns," they said, and Binns buzzed.

The procession halted at a safe distance from the study and Jennings and Darbishire walked on alone. When they

172

reached the door, Jennings said: "Go on, Darbi—bags you knock!"

"No, bags *you*!"

"One of us has got to."

"Well, you do it then. I'm not much cop at knocking on doors. I might make a bish of it."

"All right, then. Let's get it over!" Jennings tapped the panel softly and then held his breath until the summons to enter came from within.

The Headmaster's face was devoid of expression as he looked up from his desk. A bad sign, they told themselves as they waited for the storm to break; and indeed, Mr. Pemberton-Oakes had no intention of disappointing them for he was feeling particularly angry. Admittedly, the boys' actions had not influenced Mrs. Merridew, for she had made her decision before the unfortunate incident had been discovered: but on the other hand, their deliberate breaking of bounds had caused a very embarrassing situation.

The Headmaster cleared his throat. He had decided to talk for some thirty-five minutes on the error of foolish behaviour and then to drive home his argument with the cane which he kept in the corner cupboard. He stared at them in silence for some moments; then he said: "I have given some thought to your extraordinary behaviour yesterday afternoon and, frankly, I am at a loss to understand it."

"It wasn't really our fault, sir. You see . . ."

"That will do, Jennings. Actions speak louder than words and no amount of explanation will convince me that what I saw yesterday with my own eyes . . ."

At that moment the telephone rang and the Headmaster lifted the receiver. "Hallo! Linbury Court School," he said icily, annoyed at the interruption. "Yes, it's the Headmaster speaking . . . Who is that . . . Oh! hold on a moment, will you!"

He nodded an order to Jennings and Darbishire to wait outside in the corridor, and as the door closed behind them he spoke again into the telephone.

173

"Good morning, Mrs. Merridew," he said. "Roger has suffered no ill-effects, I trust?"

"Oh, no, he's perfectly well, thank you!" Diana Merridew had a pleasant voice, but even if she had croaked like a frog her next words would still have sounded as music in the Headmaster's ears. "I've been thinking things over," she said, "and I should like to send Roger to Linbury next term, if it's convenient for you to have him."

Convenient to have him! No news could have been more welcome, for now there would be no rift between the school and its most distinguished Old Boy.

"Yes, yes, of course, I should be delighted," replied the Headmaster, "but I thought—ah—from what you said yesterday I was led to suppose . . ."

"I've changed my mind," said Mrs. Merridew. "As a matter of fact it was that little scene by the pond that decided me."

"By the pond! But surely . . . !" For the life of him the Headmaster could not make sense of it.

"Yes; you see, I'd been judging the school by the parade-ground inspection you'd prepared for us. The General was frightfully pleased by it, of course, but it made me think that if school life was going to be like that all the time, it wouldn't suit a boy like Roger."

"Oh . . . H'm . . . Well, of course we *did* make a rather special effort for your visit," the Headmaster conceded. "I must confess that normally we tend to become—ah—somewhat less formal than our tour of the school seemed to indicate."

"So I gather from what Roger has been telling me. He says the boys build the most wonderful huts and have feasts in them and sail model yachts on the pond. It sounds splendid fun; and Roger can hardly wait to come to school and start building one himself."

The Headmaster's brow puckered in a frown of indecision. To explain that the huts were now a thing of the past and the pond was out of bounds would mean that the youngest Merridew would not be sent to follow in the footsteps of his distinguished grandfather. Perhaps he *had* been rather harsh in banning this innocent activity merely because Jennings' hut had collapsed at an inconvenient moment.

"I think you can rest assured, Mrs. Merridew," he replied, "that Roger will be given ample scope to indulge in suitable forms of outdoor recreation."

"That's fine, then. Oh, yes; and those two boys who organised that wonderful game of hide-and-seek for him— you won't be annoyed with them, will you? Roger says it wasn't their fault that his clothes got in that state."

Again the Headmaster pondered: then, he said: "Quite frankly, Mrs. Merridew, I had intended to punish them severely."

"Punish them! Oh, but surely they deserve a reward more than a punishment; I was going to ask you to thank them for me, because I should never have decided to send Roger to Linbury if they hadn't shown me the more human side of school life."

For some minutes after he had replaced the receiver, Mr. Pemberton-Oakes sat and stared out of the window, deep in thought. He sat so long that Jennings and Darbishire, on the other side of the door, began to wonder whether they had been forgotten.

"I wish he'd get a move on. I want to get it over as quickly as poss," whispered Jennings. "I can't think what he's doing. I heard him put the phone down five minutes ago."

"I expect all this waiting's part of the punishment," Darbishire whispered back. "You know, like the Spanish Inquisition where they keep you hanging about in suspense, and give you plenty of time to get the wind up before they get cracking with the instruments of torture. I read a story once about a chap who'd been captured by cannibals, and when they got him in the pot they were such a long time rubbing two sticks together to get the fire started that this chap would have lent them a box of matches, if he hadn't been tied up so's he couldn't move." He shook his head sadly. "Of course, he escaped in the

175

end, though. They always do in books. It's only in real life that there's no getting out of it."

The only consolation they could think of was that it was ten minutes past nine and they were missing the first part of Mr. Wilkins' algebra lesson; but this was cold comfort compared with what would be awaiting them when the Headmaster once more bade them enter.

At that moment, he did: and when the boys had ranged themselves before his desk once more, he said: "Well, and what have you two got to say for yourselves?"

Jennings caught his breath in surprise. The voice sounded so warm and friendly. Could it be a trap to lull them into a feeling of false security? Was it another method of building up the suspense like that endless waiting in the corridor? Still, the Headmaster was waiting for an answer of some sort, so Jennings said: "Please, sir, we're very sorry we made such a mess of Roger, sir."

"Ah, well, it was just an accident, I suppose," replied the Headmaster, unexpectedly. "And it's had its compensations. You'll be pleased to hear that he'll be coming to school here next term." He paused as though in doubt about what to say next.

"Yes, sir," they said, blankly. This interview was not going according to plan. They had come prepared to stop a rocket and the Headmaster was taking a very long time about igniting the fuse. Darbishire was put in mind of his story about the cannibals rubbing pieces of wood together. Should he offer to help? Anything would be better than this uncertainty!

He was just piecing a sentence together in his mind when the Headmaster went on: "I have been thinking over the whole question of these huts, and I have come to the conclusion that there is, after all, something to be said in their favour. Properly organised, they could provide excellent opportunities to develop a knowledge of woodcraft, nature study, bird-watching and—ah, perhaps an occasional picnic might not come amiss, eh?"

"Yes, sir, of course, sir, but I thought . . ." Jennings stopped, unable to make head or tail of this sudden change of opinion. But then, he knew nothing of what had been said over the telephone!

"I propose, therefore, to remove the ban which I imposed last Monday," the Headmaster continued. "Let me see, there is no cricket match this afternoon so it might be a good idea for you two boys to go over there during net practice and repair the damage to your hut which took place on the occasion of my visit."

"*Thank* you, sir . . . Thank you very *much*, sir . . . Thank you very much *indeed*, sir."

"Mrs. Merridew has asked me to express her thanks to you for the—ah—services which you rendered yesterday afternoon. Your assistance as guides had more successful results than I had at first supposed and I am cancelling my rule about the huts as I feel that your efforts deserve some recognition. Run along, now, both of you. I'm sure you don't want to miss any more of Mr. Wilkins' algebra lesson than is necessary."

Jennings and Darbishire left the study in a daze of happy bewilderment. When fortune smiled unexpectedly, it was better to accept it as a pleasant surprise than to inquire into the reasons behind it.

They walked along the empty corridor in silence, but when they were approaching Form 3 classroom, Jennings said: "You know, Darbi, I think all grown-ups are crazy. One minute they're in a supersonic bate and there's a hoo-hah going on, and then, before you know where you are, they're actually saying thank you for being decent and talking about picnics and things."

"It proves what I've always said," Darbishire returned gravely. "After a certain age, they get odd. Just because they look normal, it doesn't nesser-celery mean they're not sea-lion—er, I should say it doesn't necessarily mean they're not senile," he corrected himself. He was still feeling rather confused.

"I should think the Head's definitely senile by now. He must be well over thirty—more than that perhaps, even. Say, seventy-five or eighty!"

"Never mind, we can go and build our hut again this afternoon. Isn't it wizzo!"

Form 3 looked surprised when Jennings and Darbishire came into class wearing broad smiles of satisfaction on their faces; they were even more surprised, when, at the end of the lesson they crowded round Jennings' desk and asked him what had happened.

"I bet it hurt!" said Venables. "I bet he'd been sharpening that old cane till he'd got an edge on it like a razor. How many did you get?"

"We didn't get any. He was in rather a decent mood and he seemed quite pleased to see us," Jennings answered.

Form 3 were incredulous. "D'you mean to say you didn't get six of the best?"

"No. He thanked us for all the help we'd been."

"Rot!" said Temple. "Don't you believe him! He's just trying to be funny."

"No, I'm not. It's quite true, isn't it, Darbi?"

"Yes, and that's not all," Darbishire confirmed. "He said we could go and play in the huts again and have picnics."

Form 3 laughed merrily at this innocent leg-pull. Ah, well, they thought, Darbishire *will* have his little joke!

"I can just imagine what would happen if we believed them," laughed Atkinson. "Supposing we all ankled over to the huts, and when Old Wilkie pranced up breathing fire, we calmly told him that Jennings and the Archbeako had got together and decided to put the pond in bounds again!"

Temple said: "I dare you to try it, Atki. After all, Darbishire *did* say it was all right, so it wouldn't be your fault if there was a hoo-hah."

"No jolly fear! Let Jen and Darbi do it first."

"Yes, we're going to," said Jennings unexpectedly. "We're going over there after lunch instead of playing in the nets."

Cricket practice for the whole school was the programme that afternoon. Had things been normal, the first XI would have been playing a return match against Bracebridge School, but the mumps epidemic had disorganised the fixture list, and though all the convalescents were now back in school the period of quarantine had several days to run.

Mr. Wilkins strode round the field noting with approval that everything was under control. In one corner Mr. Carter was coaching the first XI in fielding practice and, nearby, Mr. Hind was bowling in one of the nets.

All the boys were busily occupied and the thwack of ball against bat rang out on all sides. Mr. Wilkins' satisfied glance circled the field. Then he gave a sudden start, shaded his eyes from the strong sunlight and stared unbelievingly.

Scampering and skipping happily along the path which led to the pond were two boys. The master's vast voice boomed out across the cricket field: "Jennings and Darbishire, come here!"

The happy scamperers stopped in mid-skip; then they turned and made their way back to Mr. Wilkins.

"Yes, sir?"

"Where are you two boys off to?"

"We're going over to our hut, sir."

"But, you silly little boys, the huts are out of bounds!"

"No, they're not, sir. They were, sir, but they're not now, any longer, sir," Jennings explained. "The Head gave us permission to go there this morning, or rather, he gave us permission to go there this afternoon—not this morning. Well, what I mean is, he gave us permission this morning to go there this afternoon, sir."

"Nonsense! You've been getting things round your neck, again. The Head's said nothing to me about altering the rule. Go and join that net over there and I'll give you some coaching."

"Oh, but, sir, the Head really did say we could—honestly, sir!"

"Don't argue, Jennings. I'm on duty and I've heard nothing about it, so that's that."

It was useless to protest, so the two boys followed Mr. Wilkins to a net where Temple, Atkinson and Venables were lobbing easy long-hops at Bromwich.

"Come along, Bromwich, you've been in quite long enough! Let someone else have an innings," ordered Mr. Wilkins. "Now, who shall it be?"

It was agreed that Darbishire was more in need of batting practice than anyone else and soon, padded and gloved, he was at the wicket, prodding half-heartedly at the balls which flew at him thick and fast from the queue of bowlers at the far end of the pitch.

Mr. Wilkins watched for a few minutes with mounting exasperation. Then he marched into the net and delivered a spate of good advice from behind the stumps. "No, no, no, Darbishire—that's no way to play a forward stroke. You've got about as much idea as a sack of potatoes! Hold your bat straight, you silly little boy, and don't step away to the leg every time."

"Yes, sir—er, no, sir." The batsman tried hard to cope with the good advice in the right order.

"Now, let me see you do it properly! "

"Yes, sir."

A medium-paced ball arrived and Darbishire stepped back to leg and swung his bat as though wielding a scythe. The ball passed underneath and uprooted his off-stump.

"Tut-tut-tut! " clicked the coach and clasped his brow in anguish. Then he decided to give a personal demonstration. "Come away from the wicket and give me the bat," he said. "Now, send down a good length ball, Jennings, and all you others watch closely! "

"Yes, sir," they chorused, and Darbishire retired to the bowler's end, unpadding and ungloving himself as he went.

"Now, watch carefully. I shall come right forward to it and open my shoulders and drive it over mid-on's head to the boundary," prophesied the batsman, "so all you fielders had better move out a bit deeper." He took guard, patted the pitch, glanced round and then took up a purposeful stance.

Jennings swung his arm round and round to generate the current. He was hoping to bowl what he called one of his extra special super-cracking-sonic snorters. Much to his surprise, he did! And the batsman's middle stump shot out of the ground with a sharp click and landed at the back of the net.

Mr. Wilkins was even more surprised than Jennings. "Oh! . . . H'm . . . Very good ball, Jennings," he said, while the fielders danced up and down with wild gestures of congratulation.

Atkinson rushed into the net and retrieved the stump. "It was a good ball, wasn't it, sir! Why did you let it get you out, sir, instead of clouting it to the boundary as you said, sir?"

"I—er, it took me off my guard."

"But it couldn't have done, sir. You'd just taken guard."

"H'm, yes, well now, that was a demonstration of how *not* to play a good-length ball. Just as well to show you the wrong method so that you can compare it with my next stroke which will be the *right* way."

He took up his stance again, hoping that the next delivery would be easier to cope with; and when a glance at the bowler's end showed him that Darbishire proposed bowling the next ball, Mr. Wilkins stopped worrying. At any rate, his wicket would be quite safe!

"Coming down, sir. Pla-ay!" called Darbishire, and pranced along to the crease in close imitation of Mr. Carter's bowling run. He swung his arm and gave the ball a little twist as it left his hand.

Temple was standing some ten yards outside the net in the direction of cover point. The next moment he yelled aloud as Darbishire's famous leg-spinner swung round in a semi-circle and caught the fielder on his right ear. "Ow! . . . Coo! . . . Gosh, you are a great clumsy hippopotamus, Darbi!"

"Sorry, Bod—it slipped! Did it hurt you?" inquired the bowler, unnecessarily.

"I should think it jolly well did!" He tossed the ball back and moved away in the direction of the pavilion. "I'm going to take cover before the next one," he announced in aggrieved tones. "You need a crash helmet and armour plating if you're going to stay out in the open when

Darbishire starts bowling. Let me know when the 'all-clear' goes, Bromo!"

Darbishire looked downcast as he picked up the ball. "May I have another go, please, sir?" he asked.

"Yes, Darbishire, I think you'd better," the master replied. "Just a *leetle* straighter this time, if you can manage it. Try and get it in the net, if that's not asking too much!"

"Yes, sir. Ready, sir? . . . Pla-ay!" Again Darbishire ran up to the wicket. Twelve short steps, a little jump and then, to his great delight, the ball sailed straight down the pitch.

"Oh, smashing ball, Darbi!" cried Jennings generously.

"Good ball!" called the batsman at the same moment, and stepped forward and hit it with all his strength.

Mr. Wilkins' forceful character was as evident in his cricket as it was in everything else he did. One glorious over of hard-hit boundaries was worth a whole afternoon of snail-paced scoring, in his estimation. Thus, when Mr. Wilkins hit a cricket ball, he hit it hard and true, with all the weight of his thirteen-stone-six behind it; and as he smote Darbishire's second ball he felt the exhilaration known only to a hard-hitting batsman who sees the ball soaring into the blue, far beyond the boundary.

"Oh, jolly good shot, sir!" cried all the fielders in ecstasy. "Talk about a beefy swipe!"

"Wizard drive, sir! Gosh, what an outsize clout!" came from Temple, still taking cover by the pavilion steps.

"It's still rising! Golly, I've never seen such a smasher," breathed Jennings.

Up and on soared the ball, past the other cricket nets and over the tennis courts; then, as its speed slackened and it began to lose height, they saw it disappear over the hedge of the Headmaster's garden.

Mr. Wilkins was smiling broadly. "Well, now, that's the correct method of playing a . . ." He stopped abruptly; far away, beyond the hedge came the unmistakable tinkle of a pane of glass shattered into a thousand fragments.

"Good gracious!" exclaimed Mr. Wilkins.

CHAPTER SIXTEEN

Happy Ending

JENNINGS TURNED to Darbishire and his voice was hushed with awe and wonder. "I say, Darbi, did you hear that crash just then?"

"I fancy I *did* hear a sort of musical tinkle, yes," his friend agreed.

Only too well he knew what had happened. How could he be mistaken about a sound which had rung in his ears and haunted his dreams for two whole days and nights? This time, however, it was somebody else's fault and that made all the difference in the world.

"You know, Jen, there must be something rather special about my bowling," he observed. "P'r'aps it's got some sort of magnetic attraction that only operates on cucumber frames. I've only bowled two really decent balls this term and both of them have landed up in the same place. Funny, isn't it!"

"It'll be a supersonic sight funnier in a minute," said Jennings. "The Archbeako's beetling out of his garden gate like a torpedo. I can't see his face from here, but I should say he's going to action stations for a point blank broadside!"

"Golly, poor Mr. Wilkins!" murmured Darbishire sympathetically. "He'll have to stop the rocket this time, won't he? D'you think the Head will be in much of a bate?"

"Of course he will, you prehistoric remains! If he *wasn't*, we needn't have gone to all that trouble when *we* did it. He's bound to look on it as a ghastly catastroscope—or whatever you call it, and there'll be the most frantic hoo-hah—you see if I'm not right! Good job it's Old Wilkie and not us! Come on, let's go and see what he says!"

Mr. Pemberton-Oakes seldom visited his garden on Saturday afternoons, but a thought which had lain hidden in his memory since the previous day had suddenly occurred to him after lunch. He remembered that the middle pane of the cucumber frame had borne traces of dust and small fingermarks when he had been showing the General round the garden.

Now, that was unusual and called for investigation, so he went to his garden while the thought was still fresh in his mind. Odd, he thought, as he bent down and peered at the glass. Very odd! For the dust had disappeared and the fingermarks with it. It was not until much later that he learned from Mr. Carter that the pane had been changed since last he had seen it.

This pane, also, was destined to be short-lived, for even as the Headmaster stood and pondered, a cricket ball shot over the hedge and crashed through the glass not two yards from where he was standing. Fortunately, he was not hurt, but the suddenness of the crash startled him, and he was distinctly annoyed as he retrieved the ball from the bottom of the frame and set forth across the cricket field to seek the cause of this untimely occurrence.

He soon found it. Mr. Wilkins, surrounded by a small cluster of boys, was approaching from the nets. Mr. Wilkins was a big man and the size 4 bat which dangled from his fingers looked absurdly inadequate for a cricketer of such muscular proportions.

"What happened, Mr. Wilkins?" the Headmaster inquired.

At the rear of the group Jennings nudged Darbishire as though to say: "Now for it! This is where we sit back and have a hearty laugh!"

"I'm afraid I knocked the ball over your hedge," Mr. Wilkins replied.

"Really!" The Headmaster measured the distance with his eye. A truly remarkable stroke! His annoyance vanished now that he knew the accident was not the result of stupid little boys playing too near his hedge. "My word, Mr. Wilkins, it must have been an excellent drive," he said in tones of deep admiration. "I wish I'd seen it!"

"It was a wonderful shot, sir," said Atkinson.

"I've never seen such a good hit in my life, sir," said Bromwich.

"I can quite believe it," replied Mr. Pemberton-Oakes. "I congratulate you, Mr. Wilkins. I hope all you boys were watching closely so that you could appreciate the finer points of the stroke." His gaze roamed round the group. "Perhaps one of these days, Jennings, you will be able to make a hit like that, eh—ha-ha-ha!"

Jennings gave a sickly grin and said nothing.

The Headmaster turned to Atkinson: "Go and find Robinson. Tell him what has happened and ask him to fit a new piece of glass to my cucumber frame as soon as he can."

"Yes, sir."

Atkinson sped away on his errand and the Headmaster and his assistant strolled back towards the net. "You'll be playing against the Australians, Wilkins, if you go on like this, eh! Ha-ha-ha!" And Mr. Wilkins joined in the Headmaster's hearty laughter.

For some moments Jennings was too overcome to say a word. He stood staring after the retreating backs of the masters, shocked beyond measure at the rank injustice of what he had just heard. At length he said: "Well! Did you hear *that*, Darbi? Did you ever hear anything like it? Gosh, that's the most unfair thing I've ever heard of in the whole of my life!"

"I should jolly well think it is," Darbishire agreed warmly. "It gives me a heart attack when I think of all the things we had to put up with when *we* bust it."

The long list of their misfortunes flashed through their minds; the uncertainty of Aunt Angela's crumbling memory, the shock of meeting Mr. Carter at nearly every corner, the frenzied hide-and-seek in the potting shed and the nerve-racking repair work in the attic with footsteps approaching the door.

"Yes, and now Mr. Wilkins does exactly the same thing, and instead of getting in a bate, the Head laughs like a drain." Jennings' face was flushed with resentment. "Gosh, Darbi, it must be wonderful to be grown-up—you can get away with *anything*!"

The Headmaster and Mr. Wilkins were joined by Mr. Carter when they reached the nets, and for some minutes the masters stood chatting of routine affairs while the thwack of bat against ball sounded in the background.

"I wanted to have a word with you, about Jennings," said Mr. Carter. "I put him on probation yesterday and I should like to know whether the rest of the staff are reasonably satisfied with his behaviour."

"I can tell you what *I* think," Mr. Wilkins chimed in. "I think his conduct is most unsatisfactory and shows no sign of improving. Don't you agree?"

"No," said the Headmaster, unexpectedly. "I don't agree at all, Wilkins. Both Jennings and Darbishire were extremely useful and co-operative in entertaining young Merridew yesterday."

Mr. Wilkins stared in surprise. Never before had he known the Headmaster to contradict an unfavourable opinion about those particular boys. But then, Mr. Wilkins knew nothing of the part they had played in influencing Mrs. Merridew.

"Incidentally, I told them they might go over to their hut this afternoon. I wonder why they haven't done so," pondered the Headmaster.

"That was my fault," the duty master admitted. "They did say something about it, but I thought it was some trumpery cock-and-bull story they'd made up."

"Not a bit of it! I am removing the ban on hut-building. Mrs. Merridew was most impressed when she heard that organised picnics in the huts are such a popular feature of our—ah—less formal activities."

Mr. Wilkins began to wonder whether his superior was suffering from an attack of sunstroke. "But we haven't *had* any organised picnics in the huts!" he protested.

"Exactly! But that can soon be remedied." And the

186

Headmaster strode away to the kitchen to ask the house-keeper whether she could prepare seventy-nine packets of sandwiches at short notice.

Jennings was moodily uprooting a dandelion with the toe of his shoe when Bromwich bore down upon him. "Message from Old Wilkie," he announced. "He says you can hoof over to your hut if you want to. The man's mad, of course, because everyone knows they're out of bounds."

"No, they're not! I told you this morning what the Head said." Jennings' depression vanished and the wide-awake look came back into his eyes. "Come on, Darbi, let's go and get cracking on the building programme."

The little hut was not so seriously damaged as they had at first supposed. The roof was off, of course, and parts of the walls were as pitted with holes as a colander; but most of the remnants were lying close at hand and it would not be difficult to make a workmanlike job of putting them together again.

They rooted about in the remains, salvaging what they could of their home-made furniture. A few pieces were missing and Darbishire said: "I think we ought to make an inventory first, so's we can see what we've got."

"No fear! An inventory's the one thing we can do without to start with," Jennings answered. "If we hadn't had one last time, the Head wouldn't have got stuck trying to get into it."

Darbishire made pitying noises, as though humouring a dull-witted imbecile. "Don't be such an ignorant bazooka —you can't get stuck in an inventory. It's a sort of list!"

"No, it's not. It's a place where people go and invent things. How could our small back room be a sort of list?"

"I don't know how it could *be* one, but it's *got* a sort of list all right. It's listing about forty-five degrees to star-board and if we don't get cracking and prop it up, we shan't have the place ship-shape before dark."

They worked busily for more than an hour, by which time the hut was beginning to look more like its usual self. Darbishire's watch had stopped, but keen pangs of hunger told them that it must be nearly tea-time, so Jennings trotted across to the bridge to see whether anyone was still about on the cricket field. What he saw when he arrived was so unexpected that he opened his mouth and scratched his head in bewilderment. Urgently, he called: "Darbi—quick, come here!"

"I can't—I'm busy," came the muffled answer from inside the small back room.

"But, it's urgent!"

"Yes, and so's this job I'm doing. The emergency drinking supply must have had a nest of tadpoles in it when it got knocked over; there's a plague of young frogs hopping about on the *Welcome* mat."

"Never mind that now! Come over here at once. It's important!"

Grumbling at the interruption, Darbishire made his way over to the bridge. Then he, too, stared in surprise and pushed his spectacles up on to his forehead so that his vision was not clouded by the dusty lenses. "Gosh," he gasped, "what is it—an invasion?"

Stampeding through the wood towards them came seventy-seven boys clutching paper bags and plastic beakers, while the staff followed behind at a more dignified pace. The Headmaster was making good his promise to Mrs. Merridew, and the first of the picnic teas was getting off to a good start.

Over the bridge swarmed the advance party of squatters, waving their paper bags in the air in joyous lightheartedness of spirit. Binns waved his too wildly and dropped it into the quagmire below, but Matron was bringing up the rear with reinforcements of cake and sandwiches, and Binns was spared the gruesome fate of death from starvation.

The boys crossed the bridge in single file, but when the masters arrived at the quagmire they stopped, and Mr. Carter said: "We shall have to do something about this bridge. It'll never stand your thirteen-stone-six, Wilkins."

"Leave it to me! I wasn't in the Scouts for nothing," replied his colleague, and the two masters set to work with stout branches and quickly constructed a craftsmanlike bridge which was guaranteed to bear any weight up to three hundred-weight.

The staff came across then, and wandered round from hut to hut, accepting an unwanted sandwich at one and half a slice of cake at another, so as not to hurt the feelings of their hosts.

"Sir, Mr. Carter, sir, come and have tea in our hut, please, sir," begged Venables and Temple.

"No, sir, come to mine, sir," pleaded Atkinson. "Mine's miles better! You can stand up in it, and if you go to tea with Venables, you'll have to lie flat all the time, and you'll probably get indigestion, sir."

"Oh, but, sir, ours is tons better than Atkinson's, sir!" urged a dozen voices.

"I've got an air-cushion in mine, sir—come and try it!" invited Martin-Jones.

"Don't you risk it, sir," counselled Darbishire. "I know that air-cushion. It's got a slow puncture and you'll be in a draught all the time you're sitting on it, sir!"

Robinson, the odd-job man, was kept busy running a shuttle service of lemonade jugs between the kitchen and the new bridge. It was exhausting work and the Headmaster decided that a few responsible boys could do the job equally well. He called for volunteers and was rather surprised when every one of his seventy-nine boys rushed forward to apply for a post as jug-bearer. But he was not to know that each volunteer had already made up his mind to be attacked by an uncontrollable thirst as soon as he was out of sight.

Bromwich was one of the five boys selected, and when he returned to the huts on his first trip it was noticed that, instead of a jug of lemonade, he was carrying a tank of water in which a small goldfish seemed to be practising the breast-stroke backwards. If there was a picnic going on, Bromwich decided, Elmer was not going to miss any of the fun.

When the last sandwich had been eaten and the last beaker of lemonade had been drained, the squatters returned to their pond-side occupations at the point where they had left off nearly a week before. Mr. Carter helped Jennings and Darbishire to fix the ventilating-shaft so that it would never again collapse at an awkward moment; Mr. Wilkins helped Martin-Jones and Paterson to make a rope ladder, and the Headmaster strolled round the pond, pleased at the sight and sound of so much enjoyable activity.

Outside a very small hut nestling in a clump of brambles, he came upon a sign which read *No Hawkers*, and beneath this Binns was adding a post-script in red crayon—*Privet, Keep Off*. He stopped writing when he looked up and, saw the Headmaster standing behind him, and his tongue, which had been copying each letter in the air as he wrote, now returned to its normal duties.

"Please, sir, would you like to see inside my hut, sir?" he asked in his shrill, Form 1 treble.

"I think it might be better if I didn't, Binns," replied Mr. Pemberton-Oakes. "I shouldn't like to damage your hedge—though frankly I see no sign of it."

"Which hedge, sir?"

"The privet hedge to which you allude, rather discourteously, in your notice."

The youngest boy in the school looked blank for a moment and then squeaked out: "Oh, but, sir, that spells *Private*, not privet."

"Does it, really! They must have changed it without letting me know," smiled the Headmaster. He strolled on, feeling rather surprised at himself, for he did not often make little jokes at the Form 1 level of humour.

Inside the little hut everything was in its place, thanks to the help that Mr. Carter had given with the ventilating-shaft. Darbishire spread the *Welcome* mat outside the front door and Jennings built a special shelf for the *Revenge* to stand on until they were ready to sail it again. Brand new bulrush curtains hung over the glassless windows, and Darbishire's painting of the green-faced cow watching the train cross the flimsy bridge hung in its usual place. They were proud of that picture; somehow it lent an air of culture to the homely living-room.

Jennings was feeling happier than he had done for weeks, especially now that Mr. Carter had told him that his probation was over. He glanced across to where Darbishire was shooing the last stray frog through the front door and said: "I bet you a million pounds, Darbi—well I haven't got a million pounds, but I bet you one pence—I bet you no one would have thought that we'd be sitting here enjoying ourselves, this time yesterday."

"Well, of course they wouldn't—we *weren't* sitting here this time yesterday," his friend objected.

"No, I mean this time yesterday, nobody would have thought we'd be sitting here enjoying ourselves, this time today. Everything was in such an ozard hoo-hah then, and whatever we tried to do turned out to be a bish." He scratched his nose thoughtfully. "And now look at us—sitting in the little hut, full to bursting, with Old Wilkie and the Archbeako popping in every so often to see if we're getting on all right. It's crazy, isn't it!"

Darbishire said, gravely: "That just shows you how things happen. My father says that every cloud has a silver lining, and it's always darkest just before the dawn."

"Your father thought all that out by himself?" asked Jennings, impressed.

"Yes, of course. He's always saying things like that, only you won't let me finish telling you, as a rule."

"Well, you can, this time. I'm feeling in a generous mood."

"Thanks very much. Well, what my father means is that sometimes, like, say, for instance, in our case, everything looks as black as—as black as your handkerchief"—Jennings let the insult pass—"and it's so dark you can't see your hand in front of your face . . ."

"What do you want to see your hand for?"

"You don't *really* want to see your hand."

"You just said you did!"

"Ah, but what I meant was—well, anyway, what it all

191

boils down to is that everything comes out all right in the end."

"Yes, I know what you mean," said Jennings. "It's what they call a red-letter day. The huts are put in bounds again, we have a supersonic picnic, there's no prep and the masters are in such a cracking good mood you can hardly tell they're human beings, at all!" He heaved a sigh of deep satisfaction.

It was growing late and soon the whistle would blow and the squatters would be streaming back to school and up to the dormitory; and tomorrow a new day would start, bringing new problems to face and new crises to cope with. But why worry about tomorrow? It was today that mattered and nothing could spoil that now.

Jennings glowed with quiet happiness and suddenly, for no reason that he could think of, he laughed aloud.

"What's the matter?" asked Darbishire.

"Oh, nothing! I just felt like it. You know, Darbi, when things are going well like this, I can almost believe those old geezers who come down on Speech Day and tell us that being at school is the happiest time of your life."

"Well, that's going a bit far," his friend demurred. "Let's say it's the second happiest. The *first* happiest is all the time you're *not* at school."

They fell silent then. Darbishire lay on his stomach, his elbows on the ground and his chin cupped in his hands. He was full of lettuce-and-tomato sandwich and he was feeling blissfully content.

Jennings squatted on his heels in the low doorway of the little hut, listening to the busy sounds of the neighbouring squatters. Darbishire was a good sort, he reflected, but he couldn't agree with that last remark of his. Surely there was a lot to be said for being young and being at school. Why, at times like this he could almost believe that those old Speech Day geezers really *did* know a thing or two after all!